M
TUR

Turnbull, Peter,
Deathtrap /

DATE DUE			

DEATHTRAP

DEATHTRAP

Peter Turnbull

This first world edition published in Great Britain 2000 by
SEVERN HOUSE PUBLISHERS LTD of
9–15 High Street, Sutton, Surrey SM1 1DF.
This first world edition published in the USA 2000 by
SEVERN HOUSE PUBLISHERS INC of
595 Madison Avenue, New York, N.Y. 10022.

British Library Cataloguing in Publication Data

Turnbull, Peter, 1950-
    Deathtrap
    1.   Detective and mystery stories
    I.   Title
    823.9'14 [F]

    ISBN 0-7278-5597-2

*The word "snickelway" is used with
the permission of Mark W. Jones.*

Typeset by Palimpsest Book Production Ltd.,
Polmont, Stirlingshire, Scotland.
Printed and bound in Great Britain by
MPG Books Ltd., Bodmin, Cornwall.

DEATHTRAP

One

SUNDAY, MAY THE SECOND

J ohn Smith knew what he was going to find as soon as he saw the car. By bitter experience he knew; he just knew. It was a warm morning in early May, a Sunday, he would later recall, a morning on which the pleasant weather had induced him to walk not to the newsagents in the hamlet for the Sunday papers, but further afield, to the newsagents in Whickham which would involve a two-mile walk across pleasant pastures.

He calculated that the three-quarters of an hour he'd take to do the walk would see him in Whickham just after opening time, so he would have a beer or two in the Black Swan before returning home, newspaper under his arm, possibly by a different route, for lunch and a nap in the afternoon. He was late middle-aged, some would say elderly: a hot day, a walk of four miles in total, a few beers, a roast joint of beef, were, all told, guaranteed to bring on sleep.

John Smith, wearing white trousers, a short-sleeved shirt and a canvas cricket hat, followed the path from the hamlet as the path in turn followed the tree line on the edge of

1

Whickham Great Wood. And on the walk he enjoyed observing rabbits, many rabbits, and a brace of pheasants. He followed the path as it turned to the right and drove towards Whickham and it was then, as he turned the corner, that he saw the car.

It was a small white car, which, when he first saw it, was about three hundred yards away from him and had been driven up a track that led away from the road and was wide enough to accommodate a small vehicle, and which eventually petered out to become the path that John Smith was presently walking on. From his position of three hundred yards away, being blessed with eyesight which had not failed him – unlike some of his other organs, he could see that the vehicle contained a single occupant. As he neared the car he saw that he was sitting in the driver's seat, head back, slumped to one side, his arms to his left as if clutching the passenger-seat head restraint.

It was at that point that John Smith found his mind turning, as if bidden, to previous experiences. It was at that point that he knew what he was going to find. He had been 'here' not just once before, but twice. Over a period of thirty years perhaps but, nonetheless, he'd seen it before.

Twice.

It was the way the car was parked, the manner of its parking. That was John Smith's first indication. The impression was that it had been tucked away, out of sight, where no car would normally be parked, up a narrow track, snug beneath a leafy canopy of the trees of an ancient, *Domesday Book*-mentioned wood. It was parked well out of sight, about a quarter of a mile from the road which led to Whickham, and that road was a very minor road, a very minor road indeed.

The next indication that all was not well, John Smith thought, were the doors and the windows: shut, on a very warm morning.

Finally, it was the occupant. Alone, still, utterly, life-lessly still.

So it was no surprise for John Smith that upon nearing the vehicle he saw a hosepipe leading from the exhaust to the interior of the car, via a narrow crack in one of the windows, the only window that was not tightly shut.

He stood close to the car. The engine was no longer running, but the bonnet was still warm to the touch, more so than if the morning sun alone had heated it. The vehicle, John Smith deduced, had only recently run out of fuel, but had done so long enough ago to allow the carbon monoxide to seep out of the inside of the car through the small holes in its floor and dissipate into the atmosphere. A time, he felt, that would have been measured in minutes. Not seconds, not hours, but minutes.

The first suicide that Smith had come across was a double suicide, an elderly couple who had gone to sleep holding hands. At the inquest, it had emerged that the man had been charged with shoplifting not long before his death. He was a retired senior professional, the offence was his first, and the prospect of appearing before the Magistrates was more than he could bear and so, in his declining years, he chose to take his life, leaving a note saying that his action was 'akin to catching the early bus'. His wife, who had many years earlier, when a young woman, made vows she was determined to continue to keep, had loyally remained with her husband and they entered the hereafter together, having and holding.

Fifteen years later, Smith had come across another car,

which was parked in a remote place, with a pipe running from the exhaust to the vehicle's inside. That, the second suicide, he came to consider the most distressing of the three, for in that car, in the rear seat, were two infants, buckled in safety seats, with a woman lying on her side across the front seats. At that inquest, evidence showed that the woman, the mother, was being treated for depression and her GP, fearing that she would become addicted, had prescribed only modest medication. The woman's husband, the children's father, had repeatedly warned the authorities that his wife was going to do 'something silly' but he was not taken seriously. Like all victims, she was not seen nor heard at her inquest and so no one, save possibly her husband, knew how ill she had been until she had done what she had done.

And now, fifteen years later, John Smith chanced upon his third incident of suicide by carbon monoxide poisoning. The victim, this time, was male, youthful he thought, but then Smith was sixty-seven years of age and so anyone younger than forty was young in his eyes.

He opened the car door. He was surprised that he could do that because in the other two suicide incidents, the car doors had been locked from the inside. He reached in and felt for the man's pulse. There wasn't one, nothing that he could detect. His years in the RAMC told him that this young man was beyond rescuing, that this young man had gone where he intended to go and that, by all appearances, had been ruthlessly single-minded in achieving what he wanted.

John Smith noted with some alarm that the man had chained his feet to the pedals of the car and had similarly chained his wrists to the passenger-seat head restraint, hence, he surmised, the unlocked door. It would be simple enough to do: first chain your feet to the pedals, turn the ignition on and start the car, then quickly chain your wrists to where you can't reach the ignition and snap the last padlock shut. Can't change your mind at the last minute, not once the last padlock goes 'click'. No need to lock the car door as a barrier to your own escape. Remote place, little chance of anybody finding you before the end. No escape route, not with a padlock and chain. One-way ticket.

Making sure. Making sure all right.

Smith closed the car door with reverence, slowly, but firmly, and resumed his walk to Whickham, but he no longer strolled, enjoying the morning, rather he walked urgently now bent upon a pressing errand. He no longer pondered the beauty of the Vale of York about him, but thought only about life's inevitable conclusion. He recalled how, as a young boy, he had been saddened to learn that mayfly are born and they die within a single day, but with hindsight he realised that that information had been a valuable lesson in the essentially unfair nature of life. He no longer thought of the Sunday newspapers and a pint or two in the Black Swan, his thoughts dwelt wholly upon a telephone kiosk of the modern European design, square and perspex, which stood in the centre of Whickham, and of the number nine he would dial three times, and what he would say when his call was answered.

He reached the village and walked up to the telephone box which was fortunately not in use, though had it been in use he would have had no hesitation in interrupting the caller. He entered the kiosk, picked up the receiver, dialled 999 and reported his grim discovery, adding that there was no need to hurry and that he would wait by the kiosk. He replaced the receiver and stepped out of the kiosk and stood on the grass verge and found time to observe the village: the angular tower of the parish church with the flag of St George hanging limply from the flagpole, the ducks swimming on the pond in the village green, the slate-tiled cottages, two children on bicycles, a man ambling into the Black Swan with a newspaper under his arm, exactly as he intended to do and, above all, a wide blue sky with a few wisps of cloud. He had observed this scene so many times before, but now it all seemed more real, more immediate somehow.

The area police car arrived within ten minutes. Seeing the vehicle turn into the village, Smith raised his arm and attracted the attention of the driver who flashed his headlights in response and accelerated towards the telephone box, slowing to a halt when he reached John Smith. A few words were exchanged and then he climbed into the rear seat of the car. He directed the driver to the narrow track at the end of which stood a white car in which a young man had apparently taken his life. He asked the driver to 'have faith' when the track revealed itself to go on seemingly endlessly, but eventually the small white car with the hosepipe leading from the exhaust came into view. The driver parked the car about thirty feet from the white Ford Fiesta and, without a word being exchanged, the two officers got out of the police car and walked towards the car. Smith got out of the police vehicle but, knowing his place in such circumstances, didn't accompany the constables, and remained beside the police car. He watched with interest as the officers inspected the car especially its inside. The officers returned to the police car, one leaned into the car and picked up the radio. Smith listened as the officer confirmed a suspicious death 'probably suicide', and requested CID attendance, the police surgeon and SOCO to attend. The second constable walked to the boot of the police car and removed a spool of blue and white tape which he began to suspend around the car – tying it to shrubs and stakes, which he forced into the sun-baked ground, so that the tape surrounded the car at a distance of approximately ten feet.

"You're treating it as a crime?" Smith asked the youthful officer who had radioed for assistance.

"Have to." The officer smiled warmly, although his attitude was serious. "It's a crime scene until we know otherwise." He took a pen and notepad from his pocket. "Can I take some details? John Smith is it, sir . . . no other names?"

"No, John Smith is all I need. A Christian name and a surname, all very ordinary. You know, when I was a lad the bobbies would pull me for something, ask my name, and when I gave it they'd say 'come on, son, your real one . . . I wasn't born yesterday'."

The constable smiled. "Your address, Mr Smith."

"White Cottage, Halpam."

"Where's that?"

John Smith pointed to his left. "On the other side of Whickham Great Wood. There's only a dozen or so cottages, a small shop and a small farm, and that's the hamlet of Halpam. Not many folk have heard of it, fewer still know it's there. The weather being what it is today, I decided to walk to Whickham for my newspaper and have a pint at the Black Swan, two miles there, two miles back. Just what the doctor ordered. Didn't expect to come across yon." He nodded to the white Fiesta. "But then, I've lived long enough not to be surprised. You never know what's round a blind corner, just never know. I mean there's always something round a blind corner, or there's nothing, but that's something in a sense . . . so there's always something round a blind corner."

The constable looked at Smith quizzically but said nothing in response. "What did you do when you saw the body?"

"Opened the door and checked to see if the man was still alive. I didn't think he would be. I spent seven years in the Royal Army Medical Corps. I know a dead body when I see one, but I couldn't leave him and raise the alarm without checking for a pulse . . . had to do that. Closed the door again – so my prints will be on the door."

"No worries about that, Mr Smith."

"Walked to the village, and here you are."

"And you found the body at what time?"

"I didn't check the time . . . I think it took fifteen minutes to walk into the village from here."

"We got your 999 call at five past eleven, so if we assume you found the body at ten fifty approx . . . a bit late—"

"Well, as you see, it's well tucked away, that has to be the explanation."

"Did you see anything suspicious?"

"Not a thing. I often do this walk from my house to Whickham, about twice a week in the summer and autumn, when it's dry. Keeps me fit, a walk also keeps the brain active . . . both important for a retired man."

"I can imagine."

"I was a postman for forty years, forty-two years in fact, hardly a day off sick in that time. I always have been active, active at school, only shone at sports; seven years in the army, then I was a postman for the rest of my working days. You know, this is the third time in my life that I've come across this type of suicide."

"Really?"

"Yes, first two occasions I was delivering mail, first on the scene in the early morning you see, so yes, this is a bit of a late discovery. Well, if you have no further use for me . . ."

"But there's nothing at all unusual about the scene? Apart from the obvious?"

"No. I could do this walk blindfolded. I'd be the first to notice something out of place or missing."

"Thanks, Mr Smith."

John Smith turned and walked back to Whickham. He'd come for a newspaper and he didn't want to go home without one. But he no longer wanted a beer.

Detective Sergeant Yellich was the duty CID officer that morning. Sunday morning was not usually an unpleasant shift – quiet in the main – and that morning was not out of character, with just three open incidents entered into the computer as 'complaints' still unresolved, which meant that they could not be closed. They had all been matters for the uniformed branch, nothing 'open' to the CID, so it was a morning of catching up on paperwork, writing reports, filing papers and documents rather than leaving them to languish in his in-tray. Sunday morning was pleasantly quiet – normally.

Yellich received the phone call at fifteen minutes to midday, listened to the details, wrote down the location and considered the fact that he could have been summoned to worse locations, much worse. But Whickham was up by Malton, one of the more pleasant areas covered by Micklegate Bar Police Station and the prospect of a pleasant drive to the north and east of York had its appeal, despite the tragedy that was awaiting his attention at the investigation. He arrived at the scene of the crime, as it was classified until foul play could be ruled out, at twelve thirty. The Scenes of Crime Officers followed him in their own vehicles.

Yellich saw what John Smith and the two constables had seen some thirty-plus minutes earlier: the young man with red hair and a neatly clipped beard, his eyes closed as if asleep, the chain, the padlocks and the hosepipe. Like Smith, Yellich thought that manacling oneself in such a manner was very easily done; everything fastened except the last padlock, switch on the ignition, press the last padlock shut and wait for eternity. And all the equipment – the lightweight silver chain and the small brass padlocks – could have been purchased from any do-it-yourself shop, or supermarket.

He glanced to his left as yet another car arrived at the scene. He didn't recognise the car, but the driver, a Sikh, was Dr Mann, the police surgeon.

Yellich turned again to consider the corpse. Unlike John Smith who had spent seven years in the army and the remainder of his working life at the Royal Mail and, unlike the two constables who were both very 'new', Yellich was a CID officer with well in excess of ten years experience and in those years he had developed a police officer's 'nose' for the suspicious. His experience and his 'nose' told him that this was a little too determined a suicide bid.

Too determined by half.

He brushed an annoying fly away, then stepped back and allowed Dr Mann to approach. The two men smiled warmly at each other. Yellich wondered at the discomfort of a turban on such a hot day. "Good morning, sir. One male, apparently deceased, apparent suicide."

"Well, let's see." Dr Mann approached the vehicle and examined the corpse. "Well, he's not apparently deceased, he is deceased. Death is confirmed at twelve . . ." Mann looked at his watch, "twelve forty-two in the afternoon of the second of May."

"Twelve forty-two a.m." Yellich repeated and scribbled a note in his book.

"There's no obvious indication of foul play, not that I can observe. Rigor is established . . . allowing for the warmth of the weather, I'd say that he died during the hours of darkness, but nearer dawn than dusk, though that's really the province of the pathologist. He wasn't leaving anything to chance, was he? I mean, the padlocks and chains."

"So I observe, sir." But Yellich didn't voice his suspicions. Dr Mann and Yellich stepped back to allow the Scenes of Crime Officers to photograph the corpse. Yellich looked about him, the summer baked soil of the meadow afforded no clues that he could observe – no footprints, no tyre tracks from another vehicle.

"You know," Dr Mann looked at the car but spoke to Yellich, "I've seen suicides that are even more certain than this . . . other suicides where the person was leaving nothing to chance."

"*More* certain than this, sir?"

"Oh yes. Once particularly. I remember a young man with a history of psychiatric ill health . . . went into a wood carrying a can of petrol and a cigarette lighter, a sharp knife and a length of nylon rope. He doused himself in petrol, climbed a tree, fastened the rope round his neck and tied the other end to the branch he was sitting on, slit the wrist of one hand then flicked the cigarette lighter. Remote place, self-immolation by fire, hanging, slitting wrists – all rolled into one. The flames burnt through the nylon rope so it was really the flames that killed him but not until he'd managed to run about twenty feet from where he'd landed when the rope severed."

"Hardly bears thinking about."

"Doesn't, does it? So the point is, that as determined efforts of self-destruction go, this merits a six on a scale of one to ten. It's quite determined, but only quite." Dr Mann paused but continued to look at the body.

Yellich allowed Dr Mann to hold the pause and then said, "Can I ask if you are suspicious at all, sir?"

A further pause, then Dr Mann said, "Well, in a word, yes. Yes, I am a little suspicious. I am not so immersed in police work that I subscribe to the canteen culture that 'they're all guilty unless you know otherwise' if only because the truth of the matter is that most people *are* innocent. I think that the statistic which shows that our prison population is only one thousandth of our total population should tell us that, even allowing for the number of people who escape prison because of legal technicalities. That's not me having faith in human nature, it's an easily proven matter of fact." He turned and faced Yellich. "But I also refuse to jump to conclusions. This man could easily have chained himself up in this manner but, equally, he could also have been chained up to prevent him from escaping. We don't know . . . we just don't know. Immediate impressions and overall appearances tell us nothing."

"They don't, do they, sir?" Yellich squinted against the glare of the sun.

"He's very well dressed for a suicide victim."

"Sir?" Yellich pondered the fact that he had never before considered dress to be an issue in a suicide assessment.

"I'm groping in the dark, sergeant, but . . . neatly groomed hair, trimmed beard, clothing appropriate for his age,

12

polished shoes, clean manicured fingernails, nice looking wrist-watch, a car that's clean inside and out. I mean, I'd say that this was self-respect, self-pride, I'd say that this chap was on top of his life. Such people do not easily succumb to suicidal despair. He looks like a highly unlikely suicide victim, but I have to say unlikely because that's the keyword in suicide: unlikely. It is often the most unlikely people that go to such lengths. So this may be suicide after all."

"But equally," mused Yellich, "equally, it may not."

"As you say, we don't know, sergeant. I don't want to send you down a track which doesn't exist, but equally, too rapid a conclusion at this stage that our friend here committed suicide could be deeply humiliating for us at a later date, and would allow the felon or felons to escape justice. I would suggest, with respect, that you invite the forensic pathologist to attend."

"I think I'll do that, sir."

"Do you know who he is? The victim, I mean?"

"I don't actually. But while you are here, sir—" Yellich stepped forward and reached into the inside pocket of the man's jacket and extracted his wallet.

"Well if he was murdered, it wasn't for his wallet, nor for his wrist-watch." Dr Mann observed with what Yellich took to be a sliver of humour. "That leans towards suicide."

"He was . . ." Yellich unfolded the driving licence contained in the wallet, "one Cornelius Weekes, aged – by rapid calculation from his date of birth – thirty-two years. He lived in Bishopthorpe, York. So suicide or murder, it still belongs to Micklegate Bar." Yellich poked more deeply into the wallet and found and removed an ID card showing Cornelius Weekes to have been a part-time student at the

University of Huddersfield. The photograph on the ID card was definitely that of the deceased. Yellich showed the card to Dr Mann.

"Well," Dr Mann murmured, assessing the card. "That proves his identity."

"Bad news for somebody." Yellich slipped the card back in the wallet. "Some poor soul is going to have this beautiful day ruined for them."

"Leans towards foul play."

"Sir?"

"He was doing a part-time degree, an MA, a higher degree – that's not a suicidal personality."

"It isn't, is it, sir?" Yellich tapped the man's wallet against his hand, then turned to the Scenes of Crime Officers. "Can I have a production bag for this wallet, please. Then can you please lift any latents from the car?"

Louise D'Acre followed the directions she had been given, piloting her cherished red and white Riley, circa 1947, from her home in Skelton, turning left and right, as directed, until she reached Whickham. She continued to follow directions, driving through the village and entering a narrow lane which she drove down slowly and carefully until she saw a female police officer beside a police car, who, on seeing the distinctive motor car, raised her hand in recognition. Louise D'Acre drove on until she halted by the female officer who was dressed smartly in a crisp white blouse, serge skirt and blue tights which Louise D'Acre mused must be uncomfortably warm on a day like such as this one. She wound down her window as the constable approached the driver's side of the vehicle.

"Afternoon, ma'am," the constable smiled, "the crime

scene is up the track, about quarter of a mile." She pointed to the path leading from the road and into the field system.

"Very good, I'll walk." Louise D'Acre opened the rear hinged door of the Riley and swung her legs out, both together, reaching for a black leather bag which lay on the front passenger seat as she did so. "Tell me, are you stationed here or are you waiting for me?"

"Stationed, ma'am." Louise D'Acre thought the constable to be about nineteen years old. The girl had high cheekbones, blonde hair done up in a bob, and was just a few years older than her own daughters, and doubtless she was the pride of her parents.

"In that case, I'll leave my car here with the ignition key in case you have to move it, but I don't want it driven off the road. It's a valued possession and I impose limits on its use, and driving along dirt tracks is definitely off-side, one very major 'no no'. Even if the soil is as hard as it is at the moment."

"Very good, ma'am."

Louise D'Acre walked slowly up the track, casually dressed, in jeans and a blue T-shirt. To her left was a hedgerow interspersed with shrubs and an occasional tree; to her right was a green meadow dotted with yellow clumps of buttercups. There was birdsong in the still air and, high above her in the blue, near cloudless sky, there was a vapour trail left by an aeroplane.

She saw the police activity ahead of her: two unmarked cars, a police vehicle, and a third car around which a blue and white tape had been suspended. She recognised the Scenes of Crime Officers and the plain clothed Detective Sergeant Yellich. But no Chief Inspector Hennessey – that did surprise her.

Yellich nodded reverentially as Louise D'Acre approached. "Dr D'Acre," he said. "Thank you for coming."

"As duty dictates." Louise D'Acre smiled.

Any observer would consider her a slender woman of good muscle tone, close cropped hair, black but greying slightly, and which she clearly accepted with grace and dignity. She allowed herself a trace of lipstick, but otherwise wore no make-up. Just a gentle face of clean, healthy skin and warm, brown eyes. A woman in her mid-forties, whose appeal lay in her learning and integrity. "For what am I summoned to this fair place on this fair day?" she questioned with a smile.

"A death, probably suicide, but neither myself nor the police surgeon—" Yellich stammered. "I confess, I found alarm bells ringing straight away but Dr Mann, who has pronounced the man dead and has left the scene, cautioned us not to leap to conclusions and it was he who also suggested that we ask you to attend. We are erring on the side of caution."

"I see, sergeant. Quite correct. Chief Inspector Hennessey isn't here?"

"One of his occasional weekends without duty."

"Lucky him."

Louise D'Acre and Yellich walked towards the white Fiesta.

"I was going out with Danny this afternoon."

"Danny, ma'am?" Yellich lifted the blue and white police tape as Louise D'Acre nimbly bent beneath it.

"My horse."

"I'm sorry."

"No matter. My daughters were delighted, it meant they got him to themselves for the afternoon instead of me having him. On such matters, I pull rank in our family, but Danny doesn't mind either way, he gets the gallop he loves. So what have we?"

"Male, believed to be one Cornelius Weekes."

"Lovely name. If I remember my Sunday school, wasn't he the centurion at the crucifixion who became a Christian?"

"Wouldn't know, ma'am. I just thought it was a fancy name."

"Yes."

"His driving licence says he's aged thirty-two. Hosepipe fixed, as you see, ankles and wrists padlocked. Could be a suicide."

"Yes, he could very easily have fastened himself up like that." Louise D'Acre spoke more for her own benefit. "After starting the engine and letting it idle . . . carbon monoxide is a narcotic drug, it induces sleep, and an idling engine produces more carbon monoxide than a fast revving engine. He would have been comatose within ninety seconds and deceased within ten minutes. But I see what you and Dr Mann mean. I too am reluctant to accept this as suicide." She leaned forward and examined the corpse about which a half dozen flies were by then buzzing. "Although there's going to be no doubt as to the cause of death, the pinkish hue of the skin is a clear indication of carbon monoxide poisoning, what I would expect to find is some chafing around his wrists where they have been held by the chain, suggesting a last-minute panic. You see, the will to live often reasserts itself at the last minute in suicide attempts, the lines gouged in the turf at the top of Beachy Head being a good example."

"Sorry, the what at the top of Beachy Head?"

"It's a favoured suicide spot. On occasion, folk start thinking that jumping isn't such a good idea after all, and that life and the world isn't such a bad place, by which time they're hanging on with their fingernails with seven hundred feet of daylight between them and a very hard place beneath. Such people often try to claw their way back on to the cliff top but all they manage to do is claw a few desperate lines in the turf. So, in much the same manner, I would expect to find indications that he too struggled against his shackles at the last minute but, as you see, there is no such chafing. None, no abrasions to the skin at all."

"So I see . . ."

"In itself, it doesn't mean anything, but if it were present it would indicate that he was conscious just before he died, it would at least have told us that. So, what aroused your suspicions? Yours and Dr Mann's?"

"The overall appearance of the victim: neat, well groomed, a tidy car, and an ID card to show he was a part-time MA student at Huddersfield University. He had self-respect, he had ambition. He liked himself."

"Yes, I'd go along with that. I think you're right to be suspicious, but it's not a proven case. I've attended suicides wherein the victim was all these things, but it still didn't prevent them killing themselves." Louise D'Acre moved the arm of the corpse. "Rigor is established . . . in this weather, I'd say death occurred six to eight hours ago, just before dawn; the time of the owl rather than the blackbird, the time of the badger, not the rabbit, but only just. If you've taken all the photographs you want, I'd like to remove him so I can take a rectal temperature which will help me narrow down the time of death. Then he can be removed to York District Hospital. I'll conduct the post-mortem as soon as possible."

"He'll have to be identified first, of course. Shouldn't be difficult. He's got a local address and looks as if he was socially integrated, he'll have a next of kin or some such."

In the event, Yellich found it to be quite difficult. It was not difficult from a procedural point of view. From that point of view he was ready to concede that it was a straightforward notification and identification. But, rather, it was emotionally difficult. Emotionally, it was very difficult. Perhaps it would be the most difficult experience of his career to date. He felt the woman's pain, really felt it more so than he had ever been affected by another person's emotion, save perhaps for those emotions related to his his personal life.

Cornelius Weekes, it transpired, had lived with his mother in a modest house in pleasantly suburban Bishopthorpe on the southern edge of the city of York. The front door of the house was opened immediately upon Yellich's polite but unmistakable police officer's knock: 'tap, tap . . . tap', and did so to reveal a silver-haired lady wearing a yellow pinafore over a blue dress with matching blue carpet slippers. The woman's eyes went from Yellich's solemn countenance to that of the equally serious expression of the female police constable who stood beside and a little behind him, and who earlier that day had stood watch over Dr D'Acre's Riley when she had refused to drive it off the road. The silver-haired lady gasped, her hand went up to her mouth, her eyes widened in fear, which seemed to both officers to be heading on to panic.

"Mrs Weekes?" Yellich asked.

"Yes," she said in a shaking voice. From behind Mrs Weekes came the homely smell of Sunday lunch being cooked. "Aye, I'm she."

"Mrs Weekes, may we come in? I'm afraid I have some bad news for you."

Mrs Weekes began to sink backwards. Yellich stepped forward and eased her into a sitting position on the stairs just behind her. Then she began to shake uncontrollably and let out a howl like a wounded animal.

Howled.

Howled.

And howled, so long and so loud that a concerned neighbour presented himself to see what was amiss.

"The lady's son," Yellich said to the man, who was well set with a round ruddy face, and probably in his sixties. "We haven't actually told her, we have not been able to, not in so many words. She's assumed the worse, and I'm afraid she's assumed correctly."

"Well there's only her and Cornelius," the neighbour said, a clear note of regret in his voice.

"We said we had some bad news."

"That's all you need say. It meant you hadn't come to arrest him. There's only one thing you could have meant by 'bad news', Jean's not so dim-witted."

"When he didn't come in I knew something was wrong," Jean Weekes sobbed into her pinafore. "He'd phone if he was going to spend the night out with Lucy, and anyway, she's away this weekend."

"Lucy?" Yellich appealed to the neighbour. "His girl-friend?"

"Yes. They're engaged. Nice girl, sensible."

"I see."

The neighbour pushed past Yellich. He knelt down and put a comforting arm around Mrs Weekes. "Jean," he said. "Jean, I'm so sorry." And Mrs Weekes buried her head in her neighbour's chest and wept until his shirt was saturated.

Yellich and the female constable stepped back outside the house, but remained on the step, allowing space for Jean Weekes to weep and be comforted. Eventually the neighbour pulled himself away from Mrs Weekes and stood beside Yellich. He asked what had happened to 'our Cornelius'?

"We don't know how he died."

"But he is dead?"

"Yes, I'm afraid so."

"Not badly injured?"

"No, I'm afraid not. He is dead. His body was found this morning. I'm afraid that there's going to have to be a post-mortem to determine the cause of death."

"Oh, Jean won't like that."

"I can sympathise, but it's going to be necessary." Yellich spoke as softly as he could.

"And I can understand that, but Jean—"

"I don't want to press things, Mr—?"

"Arkwright, Bill Arkwright."

"Mr Arkwright, we are certain as we can be that the deceased is Cornelius, but Coroner's Rules dictate that a formal identification should be made of the deceased by someone who knew him or her well."

"I can do that. Me and my wife have been Jean's neighbours for forty years. I mind Jean when she brought Cornelius home from the maternity hospital. His father died when he was young, only about two years old, so he was, and so I've been the nearest thing to a father for him. I had girls, so it was fun for me to take him to the football and cricket and let him show me his train set that he got for Christmas when he was eight years old. I actually bought it for him with money that Jean gave me, but he never cottoned on. Aye, I reckon I'll do. Jean, she's not up to it."

"It would be appreciated, Mr Arkwright."

"I'll just let our Bess know what's happening, get a jacket, then I'll be with you. Our Bess can stay with Jean."

"It won't be like what you may have seen on television."

"I know, I've done it before."

From that point, Yellich and Bill Arkwright walked on in silence down the long hospital corridor.

In a room at the end of the corridor, Yellich and Bill Arkwright sat on minimally upholstered benches in a sombre coloured, softly lit room. A nurse entered the room and looked at Yellich who nodded. The nurse then pulled a sash which caused two velvet curtains to open to reveal the body of Cornelius Weekes. The body had been wrapped in white bandages around the head and tucked tightly into sheets so that only his face was visible and, by some trick of light and shadow, looked as though he was floating in a black void.

Bill Arkwright groaned. Then steeling himself he said, "Yes, that is Cornelius Weekes."

"Thank you, sir." Yellich smiled and nodded at the nurse who pulled on the sash and so silently closed the curtains.

Driving back to Bishopthorpe Yellich asked Bill Arkwright what Cornelius Weekes had done for a living.

"A reporter, journalist, you know, a newspaper man, a newshound."

"Which paper?"

"Freelance." Bill Arkwright spoke in a clipped, matter-of-fact way, as if detaching himself from events. "Wanted to be a crime reporter. Told me he was working on something big. He said it would blow the Vale apart when it was exposed."

"He didn't say what it was by any chance?"

"No. Not to me anyway." Bill Arkwright looked directly ahead as though his world had changed, and had not changed for the better. He reached out and pulled the sun visor down. It was a movement which was not really necessary and Yellich, at the wheel, had the impression that the man was shielding himself from something other than the sun.

"The body is that of a well-nourished male who has been identified as one Cornelius Weekes, aged thirty-two years." Louise D'Acre was dressed in green coveralls and was wearing a white disposable head covering, which had an elasticated rim spoke for the benefit of the microphone which was positioned above the dissecting table on the end of a stainless-steel angle poise arm. She had adjusted the arm so that the microphone itself was at the level of her forehead and directly above the centre of the table. Louise D'Acre had a soft voice and found that she needed the microphone to be closer to her mouth than was normally the case for other forensic pathologists conducting post-mortems. Mr Filey, the mortuary assistant, who agreed to extend his remit to that of medical photographer when required, stood deferentially at the side of the room. Also in the laboratory, observing for the police, was Detective Sergeant Yellich.

"Immediately obvious is an increased redness of the lips and patches of lividity about the body. Have you seen this before, Mr Yellich?"

"Haven't, ma'am."

"Come and see."

Yellich stepped forward and looked at the body – with the requisite white towel draped over the genitals – of Cornelius

Weekes which lay face up on the stainless-steel table in the brightly lit room.

"The black and blue patches here, and here, and here . . ."

"Looks like he's had a good kicking."

"Is a way of putting it, but that is lividity. The cherry red colour of the lips and the pinkish colour of the skin, as opposed to the pale colour of most corpses, most Caucasian corpses, that is, and the patches of lividity, are all symptomatic of carbon monoxide poisoning."

"I see." Yellich stepped back as Dr D'Acre picked up a scalpel.

"I'm opening the chest cavity now," Louise D'Acre spoke for the benefit of the microphone, "using a standard midline incision." She drew the scalpel down the centre of the chest from the throat to the abdomen and then from the top of the abdomen towards both hips. She peeled the skin back and then, replacing the scalpel, took an electrically powered circular saw and sawed between the centre of the ribcage. She noticed Yellich grimace and told him not to worry, explaining that she and those of her kind are the few members of the medical profession who need not worry about their patient's discomfort. She then returned her attention to the post-mortem, pulling the ribcage apart she said, "I note reddening of the lungs and viscera." She took the scalpel from the instrument trolley, she placed it on the heart. "I note similar reddening of the blood in the large vessels of the heart. Death is confirmed, as initially thought and suspected, as being due to carbon monoxide poisoning." She replaced the scalpel on the instrument trolley and turned to Yellich. "The mechanism of this type of death is quite simple, you know. Blood carries oxygen around the body, carbon monoxide is more efficient at getting into the blood stream than oxygen is, and carbon monoxide will displace oxygen from the blood stream. And exposure to air containing just one part in five hundred of carbon monoxide can cause death within a few minutes. Death from carbon monoxide poisoning is often suicidal or accidental. But it's rarely homicidal."

"Really?" Yellich said by means of a response, feeling the need to say something, but Louise D'Acre's observation was, he thought, nonetheless very interesting.

"Yes, really. I don't think you're likely to come across very many murders where the murder weapon is carbon monoxide." She pondered the body. "I'll extract the brain in a minute or two. I know what I'm going to find, but there may be something else about his brain which we might not expect to find. But first, I'll have a look at the posterior aspect. Mr Filey, can you take the shoulders please?"

Louise D'Acre went to the foot of the table and grasped the ankles of the deceased. "Clockwise from your perspective; three, two, one." And the body of Cornelius Weekes, still stiff in rigor, was turned face down. "Hypostasis to the buttocks and elbows is noted," Dr D'Acre again spoke for the benefit of the microphone, "and also the ankles and soles of the feet." She turned to Yellich. "Hypostasis is caused by the blood settling and pooling according to gravity once the heart has stopped beating. The blood in his forearms and upper arms settled in his elbows, the blood in his lower legs settled in his ankles and feet, and the blood in his trunk and upper legs settled in his buttocks. He was found in a sitting position with his wrists suspended at shoulder height. The pattern of the hypostasis proves that he died in the position in which he was found. There was no suggestion of his being moved after death but, the hypostasis in the areas where it is observed, proves that he wasn't."

"Died in the position in which he was found," Yellich repeated.

"As I said." Dr D'Acre felt around the side of Cornelius Weekes' skull with latex-covered hands. "No obvious sign of injury . . . oh . . ."

"Something?" Yellich asked.

"Possibly . . . it's asymmetrical . . . his skull above the left ear is flat, so let's have a look at his skull before we extract the brain." Louise D'Acre took up the scalpel and drove an incision around the head of the deceased, fully circumventing it above the ears, and then peeled the skin back, removing the scalp, revealing the skull. "Well, as neat a fractured skull as you'll ever find. See?"

Yellich came forwards as Dr D'Acre pointed to the right side of Cornelius Weekes' skull, and noted a modest looking fissure amid a raised section of bone.

"The bleeding went inside, that's why it wasn't immediately obvious to us, or to the police. He would have suffered a subdural haematoma, blood on the brain, would have made him appear to be drunk and rendered him in a biddable-like state and would have eventually proved fatal without emergency surgical intervention. And he could not have chained himself up in the manner in which he was discovered with that injury to his head, given the effect of said injury on his level of functioning. It's also hard to see him being chained up prior to being whacked on the side of the head with what must have been a linear, rather than a blunt, instrument."

"It's doubtful he could drive a car in that state then?"

"Impossible."

"So there is the suggestion of the hand of another?"

"Oh yes, quite definitely. Such an injury could be caused accidentally, falling on to a hard edge, for example. But placing him chained up in a car, with a pipe running from the exhaust pipe to the inside in order to dress it up as suicide, makes it murder most foul. I'll extract the brain, but I should find both brain tissue damaged by contact with the blood from the blow to the head and, also, carbon monoxide damage, haemorrhaging to the meninges and cortex to name but two areas of such damage. My report will be faxed to you, but you have the nuts and bolts."

"Enough to be getting on with. If you'll sent your report for the attention of Detective Chief Inspector Hennessey."

"Of course."

"So it's murder, most foul, just before dawn today?"

"That's it."

Yellich remained, as required by law, for the remainder of the post-mortem and observed as Dr D'Acre found the damage to Cornelius Weekes' brain that she expected to find. At which point she concluded the post-mortem and Yellich returned to Micklegate Bar Police Station, entering by the public front entrance and then going through the 'staff only' door.

Some quiet Sunday.

Two

*In which Chief Inspector Hennessey assumes respon-
sibility for the investigation and has reason to re-think
his opinion of a once respected colleague, and
Sergeant Yellich is supportive of his exhausted wife,
both of whom are 'at home' to the gentle reader.*

George Hennessey relaxed in his chair, sitting back.
Occasionally he would glance out of the window of
his office as he noticed a sudden movement or a bright
colour, and then he'd see a group of tourists walking the
walls or a cream-coloured open-topped double-decker bus
sweeping by. But not once did his mind lose its focus on
Detective Sergeant Yellich's feedback.

He glanced at the Police Mutual calendar on the wall
beside his grey steel filing cabinet as Yellich's report drew to
its conclusion. "Thank you," he said. "That was an excellent
feedback."

"Sir." Yellich smiled, mollified by the compliment. He
watched as Hennessey swept a liver-spotted hand through
his silver hair which sat atop a wide face, which Yellich
found to be of warm countenance. Yellich had grown to
enjoy working with the Chief Inspector, and discovered that
he was learning much from him, such as the importance of

recognising and acknowledging good pieces of work, when appropriate.

"So." Hennessey leaned forward and rested his elbows on his desktop. "A mystery emerges. Or does it?"

"Sir?"

"Well, it would strike me that Cornelius Weekes' urge to be a top-flight investigative reporter caused him to stumble upon something, and that that's the mystery, Yellich. It would strike me that the key to unravelling the mystery would be to pick up his trail. What did you say that he allegedly told his father figure, the neighbour, Bill . . . ?"

"Arkwright."

"Yes . . . Bill Arkwright. What was the expression used?"

"Blow the Vale apart."

"That's it. He'd stumbled upon something that would 'blow the Vale apart'. And it cost him his life. So he knew something, and someone knew that he knew, and, as I said, it cost him his life. A little learning is a dangerous thing all right. He was about to blow the whistle on something, and someone who had a vested interest in the matter, made sure he didn't blow said whistle."

"Looks like that, sir."

"So, what was he working on? That's what we've got to find out."

"What indeed?"

"That'll be our number one priority. Pick up the trail where he left it. What are your thoughts about the murder, I mean motive aside?"

"Well . . ." Yellich paused, "having thought about it overnight, I'd say it was bungled, utterly so. A bit of a panic-driven job."

"That would be my assessment too. I don't think we're

dealing with professional criminals here. If he had been iced by professionals, his body wouldn't have been found. This would be a missing person's file, not a murder investigation.

"Reaching a little far ahead aren't you, sir?"

"Probably, Yellich, probably, but probably not." Hennessey leaned back in his chair, held eye contact with Yellich, paused, and then repeated with a smile "but only probably."

"Sir?"

"Well, we dismiss the murder being the work of pros, agreed?"

"Yes, sir."

"The appearance of the victim as being a casualty of suicide was as you first thought, 'too determined by half'. So, given that the murder was not carried out by a pro, we must assume that the killer is in the mainstream of society, and is anxious to remain there. But one thing seems sure – the murderer is in possession of a dark and dreadful secret, so dark and dreadful that he is prepared to take life in order to stay hidden."

Yellich smiled. "That's called psychological profiling, sir."

"It is indeed. It's a new term for an old method of police thinking. The Famous and Fayre is an ancient city. There's a lot of old money hereabouts, and that means a lot of skeletons in a lot of cupboards."

Yellich pursed his lips. "I want to add to your psychological profiling, sir, if I may."

"Please do, Yellich."

"Well, they didn't know their victim, or he or she didn't know his or her victim. What I mean is that Weekes was ambitious; part-time study for a higher degree, wanting to carve a solid niche in journalism, in a steady relationship – not at all a candidate for suicide. Whoever murdered him could get close enough to do what they did, but they weren't close enough to know his personality. If they knew the man, they'd have known that he wasn't a suicidal-type."

"Good point. 'They' or 'he' or 'she', though no indications that it was a conspiracy, not yet. So, what were his last known movements? Lifestyle?"

"Lifestyle, lived with his widowed mum, not a homeboy, though, in a steady relationship, like I said, stayed out overnight on occasions. But she was away this last weekend, so this last weekend he was at home with mum. On the last known movements, I'm in the dark. Only his mum could tell us that and yesterday she was in no condition to give such information."

"Fair enough."

"And, in fairness to myself, when we saw her, we were still considering the suicide angle so I didn't press for detailed information."

Hennessey nodded and inclined an open palm towards Yellich. "Again, fair enough, but that'll be our first port of call, then the girlfriend . . ."

"Lucy. By name," said Yellich.

The front curtains of the house were shut. A solemn recognition of a death in the household, a recognition which George Hennessey had first encountered in his boyhood home and recalled seeing often in his youth. But it was rarely observed, rarely seen, these days. The practice was a relic of an earlier era.

31

Hennessey and Yellich spoke to Mrs Weekes in the rear room of the house, where the curtains were open and looked out on to a small, but lovingly tended garden. Mrs Weekes had bravely collected herself in the twenty-four hours since Yellich and the female officer had broken the news to her of her son's death. Now she seemed to be a woman of steel.

"You're right." She glanced away from Hennessey and looked at the empty fire grate. "Cornelius wouldn't have taken his own life. He was looking forward to the future so much. He and Lucy were planning a life together, he was doing a course in history at Huddersfield, over an hour's drive each way, but he was sticking at it, got that from his father, Harry 'The Dog' Weekes. It wasn't an unkind nickname. Someone once said he had dogged determination. Cornelius was like that, once the bit was in his teeth, he was unstoppable. And he was getting on in newspapers. He had everything to live for."

"Any enemies that you know of? Any death threats?"

"No, none that I was aware of, but our Cornelius wouldn't tell me such things anyway."

"Mr . . . ?" Hennessey turned to Yellich, "The neighbour?"

"Arkwright, sir. Bill Arkwright."

"Bill," Mrs Weekes smiled. "A good friend as well as a good neighbour."

"Mr Arkwright apparently informed Sergeant Yellich here that Cornelius was working on a project which sounded quite important – seriously so – something that was going to expose some scandal in the Vale . . ."

"Well, Bill knows more than me," Mrs Weekes cut Hennessey off, clearly anticipating him. "We were close as mother and sons go, but not that close. The days when

Cornelius would come and tell his mother everything that had happened that day are long gone. Aye . . . long gone."

"We feel that it would point us in the right direction."

"Probably would, he wouldn't be the first reporter whose got too close to a story for his own good, too close for someone's comfort."

"Does he work at home?" Hennessey grimaced. "I'm sorry. Did he work at home?"

"He has a computer in his room."

"May we . . . ?"

"Aye."

"We'll go up in a minute."

"His is the front room. The curtains are shut, you'll have to switch the light on."

"Thank you. When did he leave the house?"

"For the last time you mean . . . Saturday evening. I was surprised that he went out, Lucy being away for the weekend, normally he'd spend the day and the evening at home, watching television with me, to see if he'd won the lottery. We each put a pound on it each week."

"But he went out?"

"Yes."

"How did he seem?"

"Eager, enthusiastic, as if the person he was meeting had something Cornelius wanted. It was probably the other way round, the person he was meeting wanted something Cornelius had, and that was Cornelius's life. And he took it."

"It's not safe to jump to conclusions, Mrs Weekes."

"Oh, I think it's safe to jump to that conclusion. I think it's very safe."

Yellich, sitting back to observe, read the room. It was

neat, well ordered, homely, warm – emotionally speaking: A print of a pastoral scene above the fireplace, a cabinet with hardbacked books, *Reader's Digest*s on the coffee table. A scent of wood polish and air freshener about the room. There was nothing, nothing at all, he thought, about this house and this household which would be of interest to the police. Or to cause concern, save, of course, for the dreadful matter in question. In fact, Yellich pondered, this house would make good approved lodgings for a bachelor constable – had the circumstances been different.

"It was unexpected," Mrs Weekes said. "He got a phone call on Saturday about five p.m."

Yellich and Hennessey glanced at each other.

"Do you mind?" Yellich stood and pointed to the hallway where the telephone stood.

"Won't help," Mrs Weekes smiled, again anticipating the police, "news has spread, friends and relatives have been phoning me. If you dial 1471, you'll get the number of my pal Molly in Richmond. She phoned just before you gentlemen arrived."

Yellich resumed his seat. "You don't have a caller display system?"

"No." Mrs Weekes once again turned her stare to the empty fire grate. "I don't know what one of those things is, but I haven't got one because I haven't got any fancy gadgets on the phone, not even an answer-machine."

"I don't think the technology exists to trace the calls beyond the last call received." Yellich addressed Hennessey. "Not without a caller display unit which records the number of the last thirty calls received, or without a pre-arranged trace."

"It doesn't," Hennessey replied. "I've bounced a ball down that alley before."

"He might have told Lucy," Mrs Weekes offered. "He'd tell his girl things that he wouldn't tell me – man of his age – she'd be a better source of information than I'd be, I should think."

"Where can we contact her?" Hennessey asked while out of the corner of his eye he saw Yellich open his notebook.

"I don't know her address. Her name is Lucy Gillespie. She's a school teacher, Hays Middle School in Beverley. History. It was Lucy who encouraged Cornelius to do his MA. She re-awoke his interest in things past, in days gone by. Lovely girl. She's at home today, too upset to go into school. She's phoned me, we had a chat, we needed to."

"Does she live in York or Beverley?"

"In York. Her address will be in the address book Cornelius has. He keeps . . . kept it on his desk, by his computer."

Cornelius Weekes kept a neat and tidy bedroom. A single bed against the wall, a desk and table side by side, an upright chair in front of each, papers on the desk and a Pentium P120 with printer on the table. The electric light threw a harsh light and Hennessey felt the urge to open the heavy curtains. He went to the desk and picked up the address book and found Lucy Gillespie's address under 'L' not 'G' as he had expected. But the address was clear, Buckingham Street, York. Off Skeldersgate, within the walls, and conveniently close to Micklegate Bar Police Station. Nice address, not bad for a school teacher. Manageable, he thought, salary wise, but only just.

Yellich moved to the computer and switched the machine on. It was an outmoded machine and it took a minute or two to warm up. He got as far as 'enter password' and said, "I knew it couldn't be that easy."

"See if Mrs Weekes knows." Hennessey continued to turn the pages of the address book.

Yellich left the room and returned a few minutes later and began to tap the buttons of the keyboard. "No," he sighed, "access denied. She doesn't know his password so I asked her if he had a favourite turn of phrase and the name of his teddy bear or any other unique word which held special significance. She suggested a couple of words which the machine won't recognise. I've just tried 'Lucy'. No joy."

"Write it backwards," Hennessey suggested, very pleased that he didn't belong to the computer generation.

Yellich did so, then tried Lcuy and Lycu . . . without luck. "It won't be that simple, boss, never is for me."

"Ah," Hennessey glanced sideways and smiled. "Think lucky and you'll be lucky. An elderly Quaker lady once told me that. Never marry for money but go where money is. She told me that as well." He opened one of the drawers in the desk and extracted a cardboard 'wallet' folder. Inside the folder he found a series of newspaper cuttings in respect of a murder, a conviction for murder and a report about the failure of an appeal against. "What have we here?" he said aloud.

"What's that, boss?" Yellich stood beside Hennessey.

"I remember this case . . . wasn't involved, but I remember it. Before your time, Yellich, you'd be a schoolboy at the time. One Melanie Clifford, shot her love rival, they found the murder weapon in her car. She had motive, she had the means and she was virtually found holding the smoking gun."

"Open and shut case."

"So the jury believed. She collected a life sentence. Appealed against it, lost the appeal and is still a guest of Her Majesty. Durham, I think."

"Not one of the more comfortable nicks, especially for women."

"It's not Ford Open Prison, that's for sure. You have to be a serious felon to get into Durham. But then it's not meant to be a holiday camp and she did blow the other woman's brains out, just a few months after the victim married the man who had promised to marry her. Spiteful is just not the word. Remember when your marriage was just a few months old; that lovely, beautiful honeymoon period, and imagine an old girlfriend coming to your home and blowing Sara's head off with a twelve bore. Imagine what that would do to you. No, Melanie Clifford is very well tucked up."

"So why Weekes' interest?"

"Beats me." Hennessey replaced the folder.

"Not taking the cuttings, boss?"

"Why? We'll pull the case record from the void. It'll tell us more than these can, and even then it may not be relevant. The case may have nothing to do with Weekes' murder. It was John Cross's last case, last big case anyway. I was pleased that he got a conviction, it was a good note to end on. I'd like to leave the force like that – a really good one, a very clever conviction – before the pension. Won't be long now either."

"I remember the name, John Cross. Every organisation has one or two 'names' that reach the ear of everybody else in the team. I never met him though, I was at Wetherby then. A copper of the old school, they say."

"Do they? Did they? What's the old school, Yellich?"

"A bit . . . well, guilty until proven innocent."

37

"Well, make up your own mind about folk, Yellich, don't allow others do to if for you. What I remember about John Cross is that if he saw guilt it was no mirage, it was there. He could see it when others couldn't and he was always proved right by subsequently unearthed evidence. So I'm not about to have a convulsion of guilt about little Miss Clifford. Five feet nothing in her cotton socks and every inch an evil inch. 'If I can't have him, you can't either', that sort of woman, and John Cross put her away. She deserved to be put away."

Hennessey and Yellich, both, found that they liked Lucy Gillespie. She was, they thought, bonny without having classic fashion-model beauty; attractive without being glamorous. And, though at that moment, she was clearly very distressed a genuineness, a sincerity, a glow of warm personality, was nonetheless evident. She was a short woman: who had a mop of ginger hair and a well-balanced slightly freckled face. She was a woman who liked herself without being arrogant, a woman who would transmit her appeal to others, a woman whose approval others would seek. She was, thought Hennessey and Yellich, a natural teacher of children. Neither man would have been anxious about any child of theirs being in this woman's supervision. Her small terraced home spoke of warmth; plenty of wooden surfaces, both stripped and polished, reed mats on the floor and a woven rug employed as a wall-hanging amid prints of the Impressionists. A framed photograph of Cornelius Weekes and her — in a green T-shirt, blue jeans and open-toed sandals — smiling, clutching each other was a cruel reminder of happier times, much happier times.

"I still can't believe it." She glanced out of her front window at narrow Buckingham Street and the house opposite, also of modest proportion, and also in a similar neat terrace. "Cornelius's mother phoned me yesterday, as soon as I got back in, she knew when I was expected."

"You've been away for the weekend, I gather?"

"Nottingham. Visiting my sister. She's just had her first baby, a boy. They want to call him Robin, a bit ill-advised I say for any man-child associated with Nottingham, but they're adamant. One leaves as another arrives. I still can't believe it. I was too distressed to go into work today. You're allowed one week's bereavement leave, hence the casual dress. I phoned Mrs Weekes this morning, but she didn't seem to want to talk. I mean talk on an emotional level, she was all practicalities; the funeral arrangements and so on, and that's how she'll handle things, bottle it all up, she's of that generation. You know, I don't think that she properly grieved for her husband. I got the impression that she was once spoken to very strongly along the lines of pick-yourself-up-and-pull-yourself-together-and-get-on-with-it. So she did and she has done. But that's the wrong attitude. I'm not going to be like that about Cornelius, and I'm going to make sure she isn't. It's important, nay vital, to recognise emotion for what it is and to express it. But right now I just feel numb."

"I'm sorry if this is a bad time, Miss Gillespie, but in a murder case—"

"So it was murder." Lucy Gillespie looked up at Hennessey with round brown eyes. Hennessey had sat down, as invited, in an armchair. Yellich had gingerly occupied an armchair which he doubted would hold his weight, while Lucy Gillespie had lowered herself cross-legged on to a large, dark green scatter cushion and rested her back against the wall, under a print of Monet's 'Waterloo Bridge'. "When I talked to Mrs Weekes this morning, all she said was that the death might be suspicious, or something like that. She wasn't making a great deal of sense about it, bottling it up, but not making sense either. I don't think she'll last now, not that woman. She lived for Cornelius. He was all she had. But anyway, I knew that Cornelius wouldn't take his own life. I just knew. He was on the threshold of good times, by which I mean achievement, not indulgent partying."

"So we believe, but the reason we want to talk to you is that this is a murder inquiry, the first twenty-four hours of which are the most important. We are really very anxious to get into his computer. You wouldn't know his password, by any chance?"

"No, I wouldn't. Sorry. And you won't find it by doing what they do in the television dramas, by typing in a pet word or favourite turn of phrase. That's the stuff of fiction. In reality, most people's passwords are so obscure that not even their partners could guess them. My sister's password for her computer system for instance, is based on her birth date. She was born on the seventh of August so her password is based on 'seven, eight'. She's added one to each to make 'eight, nine', which is as far as she'll tell me because she's protected it further by transposing two of the letters in each word. And that information she keeps to herself, even though without the transposition, the password is obscure enough to be safe. It just numbs your brain trying to work out the number of permutations if any four letters in 'eight, nine' are transposed in any order.

"My code word is a small town in the Canadian Prairie Provinces. I have no connection with it, or even with

Canada. What happened is that I opened the atlas at random, it fell open at North America, I closed my eyes and put a finger on the page, looked for the nearest town with more than six letters in its name, chose that for my password and then belt and bracered it by following my sister's example of transposing two of the letters. I have to do that because I keep the password's original spelling written down near my computer, but only I know its version after two of the letters have been swapped round. All I worry about is amnesia." She forced a smile.

"Point taken."

"So you won't be able to access Cornelius's system. He told me once that his word was an old English word he'd rescued from obscurity and he'd also transposed two letters. So if you programme a computer to try every word in the English language as the password to Cornelius's system, it still couldn't be found."

"Again, I take your point."

"So there's no access to Cornelius's computer for you gentlemen, nor for me. I only wish there was. Is it true that Cornelius's murder was made to look like suicide? It was on the news. I also read that in the *Yorkshire Post*. Mrs Weekes also indicated that it had been dressed up to look like suicide."

"Yes. It's true. We can tell you that."

"I knew that his wise would be his undoing." She signed and glanced round the room. "I just knew it. He's not got the bottle, he's not macho enough to do what he wants to do. It's too dangerous."

"What was his wise?"

"Ferreting away, always turning over stones – searching for what lies beneath, searching for what lies beyond. He once told me that each time you go into a new situation, there's always more than first meets the eye, and what you don't see is invariably more powerful than what you do see. If you see a calf, look for the cow, it'll be there in some guise or another. That was Cornelius. It's a wise that can carry you a long way if you're a researcher at a university or if you're a police officer, but if you're a freelance journalist without an organisation to protect you, it's a wise that can . . . well, it can be your end. As it seems to have been with Cornelius."

"Bill Arkwright the neighbour . . ."

"Yes, I know Bill. Nice chap. He was good for Cornelius."

"He said that Cornelius told him that he was on the verge of exposing something that would be quite a scandal in the Vale of York."

"Did he? Confess – if Cornelius said that then it was uncharacteristically loose-tongued of him. He always played his cards very close to his chest. But then Bill was like a father to Cornelius and maybe that could explain it. In fact it would, we all have need of an authority figure that we can trust, and Cornelius would have seen Bill Arkwright in that light."

"We had a look in Cornelius's bedroom and found some newspaper cuttings about an old murder case."

"Oh, yes . . . Melanie Clifford."

"Yes. What do you know about the case? What was Cornelius's interest in it?"

" 'Not much' and 'I don't know the full extent' would be my answers to those questions, in that order, and his interest in the Melanie Clifford case may not be relevant to his murder."

"Yes, we have allowed for that, but even so, what was

it about the Melanie Clifford case that interested him? Do
you know?"

"Her innocence."

Hennessey and Yellich walked the short distance from
Buckingham Terrace to Micklegate Bar Police Station,
entered by the 'staff only' entrance, signed in and checked
their pigeonholes. Both had received circulars to be read and
digested and then placed in the pigeonhole of the officer
whose name occurred next on the list. They walked together
to the CID corridor and then left each other's company, each
going to his own office.

Yellich, having agreed to write up the two visits made
that morning, sat at his desk, opened the still very slender
file and picked up a ballpoint pen.

Hennessey in his office, sat at his desk, pondering, and
then picked up the phone and jabbed a four-figure internal
number.

"Collator," snapped an efficient, youthful voice.

"DCI Hennessey."

"Sir?"

"Access a file for me. It'll be listed under . . . it'll be listed
under . . . you know, I can't remember the name of the
deceased, but the convicted person was one Melanie Clifford."

"I can find it from that, sir."

"Good man."

"Do you have a date, sir?"

"No . . . about fifteen years ago though, that sort of
timescale."

"I'll get right on it, sir."

"Thanks. No hurry, I'm out for an early lunch."

*   *   *

Hennessey signed out and walked the walls to Lendal Bridge and then into Lendal. The fish restaurant was crowded and so he continued into Stonegate and to the Olde Starre Inne 'York's oldest pub', which was accessed by a shaded snickelway to a cool courtyard and then to the pub proper. It was pleasantly dim inside, dark colours, a low ceiling and a few harsh lights – much to his liking. He enjoyed a pleasing lunch sitting in a corner snug beneath a framed print of a map.

The West Ridinge of Yorkshyre
with
The Moft Famous and Fayre
Citie Yorke defcribed
1610

Calmed and replenished by good fare, he returned to Micklegate Bar Police Station, retracing his steps – although on his return journey, he shared the wall with a group of junior school children, all, he thought, thoroughly well behaved.

Hennessey enjoyed the shapes of the buildings around him, a grey urban landscape of walls and roofs all to the human scale with the Minster dominating the townscape just as it should. He left the wall at Micklegate Bar and, as he did so, he spared a compassionate thought for Harry Hotspur who, centuries earlier, had been beheaded for treason and whose head had been impaled on a spike above the Bar and thus left there for three years as a warning to all who would defy the Crown.

Entering the police station, he found a memo in his pigeonhole. The case file he requested had been retrieved from the void and was presently with the collator. He walked to his office and picked up his phone and pressed the collator's number.

"Collator's department," a female voice answered.

"Where's the collator?"

"At his refreshment, sir."

"Oh . . . yes. DCI Hennessey here. You have a file for me?"

"The Erickson murder, sir?"

"Erickson. That was the name. Yes, can you bring it up to me, please. I'm in my office. Who am I speaking to?"

"WPC Wakefield, sir."

"Very good, Wakefield, bring it up." He replaced the phone, slipped out of his jacket and hung it beneath his hat on the coat stand. WPC Wakefield, when she arrived – carrying a thick file from which dust had been clearly wiped with a damp cloth – revealed herself to be a slender woman with dark brown hair and an alert and serious attitude. "The file, sir," she said.

"Leave it on my desk, please." Hennessey poured granules of coffee into the bottom of a huge mug.

"Will that be all, sir?"

"Yes, thank you." Hennessey added milk to the granules and filled the kettle. Mug of coffee in hand, he returned to his desk, sat in his chair and, leaning back causing it to creak, he picked up the file on the murder of Charlotte Erickson, for which Melanie Clifford had been convicted.

The first thing which struck him was the old-fashioned front sheet and continuation sheets, now out of date and replaced, although they had done the job perfectly well. But the illusion of progress, he often somewhat cynically felt, was always needed. The notion of 'if it ain't broke, don't fix it' had yet to, he believed, penetrate police thinking and so, every five years or so, newly designed forms were introduced giving a lovely feel of progress and forward motion whilst in reality, they did nothing more than confuse the staff. So 'Old' George Hennessey believed. But here were old forms, and he was suddenly transported back in time: a pre-teenage son who wanted to be an astronaut and a mortgage finally 'cracked'. Settling in the chair, and also settling into visions of the past, enjoying what he believed people called a 'time-warp', he began to focus his mind, glancing up once, as he sipped the coffee, at the high, blue sky above the steeply angled rooftops. He then looked at the file and began to read.

Eighteen years. How time flies, he thought, 'tempus fugit' and pondered how one m'learned son had told him that the phrase meant time running away, as in fugitive, not flying as in taking to the air. Well, well. Latin was not on the syllabus at Trafalgar Road School, Greenwich, fifty plus years earlier. Hennessey was immensely proud of his son. Immensely so, as any father would have been when he saw his son for the first time in his wig and gown. And that moment, fleeing or flying be damned, that wonderful, precious moment, that seemed like yesterday.

But time had not gone quickly for Melanie Clifford, though Hennessey didn't feel a morsel of pity for the woman. She was alive, which could not be said for her victim. But this case, this recently-wiped-off-dust file, had held a fascination for Cornelius Weekes. And that fascination just may have led to his murder.

The nuts and bolts of the case were just as Hennessey had recalled earlier that day. Melanie Clifford had had a long-term relationship with Toby Erickson. He had broken off the relationship and then a few months later, three to be exact, he had married Charlotte Erickson on one fine August day. Then, the following January, Charlotte Erickson was dead, shot once in the head, and the murder weapon, a rifle, was found in the boot of Melanie Clifford's car. Strong motive, the bitterness of a scorned woman and the smoking gun, if not actually in her hand, then in the boot of her car.

Melanie Clifford had pleaded 'not guilty'. She had, she had claimed, gone to the Erickson house in response to a phone call from Toby Erickson, who asked her to visit. So she did. When she arrived, she found the house in darkness, not even the dogs were barking which she found strange, but not, she said 'alarmingly unusual'. She had left her car at the front of the house and had walked round one side, to the rear of the building. She couldn't see anybody, despite circumnavigating the entire building, and so returned to her car. When she got home, she was puzzled and curious and was awoken the next morning by police knocking on her door and demanding to see the inside of her car. She was happy, in a bleary-eyed sort of way, Hennessey assumed, to hand over her car keys. The police opened the boot of her car and she was arrested, never again from that day to this, to return to her house.

Melanie Clifford was then charged with the pre-meditated murder of Charlotte Erickson. The jury didn't believe her story and the judge railed against her for the 'spiteful act' of taking a young life 'at the very start of wedded happiness', and had sentenced her to the mandatory term of life imprisonment, but recommended that she serve a minimum of twenty years before being released. 'You are a truly evil person. Go down'.

She had appealed against conviction. That astounded Hennessey. The case against her seemed watertight, he felt that an appeal against sentence would have been more appropriate: a woman betrayed, driven to avenge herself when in a state of emotional turmoil, now in deep remorse. Perhaps with luck and a more magnanimous panel of Appellate Court Judges, she could have won a significant reduction in her sentence. She *was* guilty of murder and an appeal against sentence would have been an implicit acceptance of that guilt. In such circumstances the 'life' sentence would have remained but the recommended twenty-year minimum would possibly, nay certainly, have been quashed. With good behaviour, clear remorse, acceptance of her guilt, she could have walked after less than ten years and so escaped institutionalisation. She could have picked up the pieces of her life and that, Hennessey believed, would have made sense. Especially since she was no spring chicken when she went inside. Thirty-seven years old when she had committed the crime, she's now – he calculated without the help of one of those infernal calculators – now she is fifty-five. So why, why, the ill-advised appeal against conviction? He sipped his coffee. There was of course only one answer and Lucy Gillespie's words of earlier that day chimed in his mind.

Her innocence.

Hennessey looked over the statements, searching for details. The incident had taken place in January of that year, specifically the eleventh of that month. Mid-week.

Dark, cold and wet, as are the winters in the Vale, but comparatively mild because the photograph showed a landscape without snow.

Melanie Clifford had a house in Fulford, at an address Hennessey knew to be council accommodation; modest living, comfortable, warm, dry, but modest. Charlotte Erickson's address was 'Coles Copse Farm', Malton. Hennessey wrote the single word 'money' on his notepad. Malton was old money, lots of it, mostly from the farming of very large farms. Fulford's income base was humble by comparison, low-income wage earners in the main. Not a lot of traffic between Fulford and Malton, he thought, not a lot of traffic at all. So that was a puzzle. He also found it difficult to believe that a man would summon a rejected lover to his house a few months after his marriage to another woman – he glanced at the front sheet – another, much younger woman, on one January night, which would involve the woman undertaking a thirty-mile round trip at ten p.m., and he further found it difficult to believe that a rejected lover would accede to such a request.

He sat back in his chair, again causing it to creak. No wonder, he mused, no wonder the jury didn't believe her, and the Appellate Court Judges either. It was, however, much more believable that a woman, at thirty-seven years of age, desperate to marry before it's too late, should begin to hate the woman in excess of ten years her junior, whom her wealthy boyfriend had rejected her for and, that burning up with emotion, she had driven out to Coles Copse Farm one dark winter's night and shot Charlotte Erickson in the head. Contemplating that, Hennessey began to doubt Melanie Clifford's innocence and was swayed once more to embrace the safety of her conviction. Nevertheless, he read on.

The police had received an anonymous phone call at six-thirty a.m. the following day, the twelfth, a Friday, informing them that Charlotte Erickson had been murdered and that the murder weapon was to be found in Melanie Clifford's car, specifically in the boot of the same. The caller also informed the police of Melanie Clifford's address. The police followed up the phone call by a visit to Coles Copse Farm and found Charlotte Erickson's body in the shrubbery beside the front door of the house. The prosecution alleged that Melanie Clifford drove to Coles Copse Farm, shot Charlotte Erickson, dragged her body into the shrubbery and then drove home, intending to dispose of the murder weapon at a later date. Toby Erickson was at a business conference in Edinburgh all that week, his alibi was sound, and it was further alleged that Miss Clifford's knowledge of Toby Erickson's business arrangements meant that she would have been aware of his movements that week. She would have known that he wouldn't be at the house and so could more easily have committed the murder. The phone call to the police was made by a male, but the recording was perfunctory, no indication of whether the caller was young, old, agitated or calm, or of what social class. Neither was the name of the constable who took the call recorded, so brains, even eighteen years on, could not be picked.

A knock on the frame of the door to his office disrupted Hennessey's concentration. He glanced up. DS Yellich stood on the threshold of his office, a piece of notepaper in his hand. "The Forensic Science lab at Wetherby, skipper. They've phoned us with the preliminaries."

"That's quick."

"Well, it's a murder, skipper, recent, A1 priority."

"Even so . . . well?"

"No prints on the car at all, save for those on the door handle of the driver's door which will doubtless be those of the fella that found him – they'll visit him to take his prints for elimination but, other than that, it was wiped clean. Inside and out."

"Interesting, but it really only serves to reinforce what we already know, that the hand of another was involved. Where exactly was the body found?"

"In a field, a long way from the road, near the village of Whickham."

"Which is where?"

"Near Malton, skipper."

"Malton?"

"Yes, is that significant?"

Hennessey patted the file. "Could be. Could very well be." He paused. "You see, this is the file on the murder of Charlotte Erickson. The woman whom Melanie Clifford was convicted of murdering."

"Cornelius Weekes was interested in her. I mean her conviction."

"Yes, professionally speaking, she was of interest to him. The murder took place at the Ericksons' home, which sounds as if it was a farm, but which is near Malton."

"Ah ha . . ." Yellich raised his eyebrows. "Anything of particular interest leap out of the case at you?"

"Nothing that screams innocence. Yet. A harsh sentence but an appeal against conviction, not against sentence."

"Interesting, skipper. I would have thought—"

"Exactly." Hennessey picked up the file. "I would have thought as well. Still, I'll press on, see what I find." He recommenced reading as Yellich walked quietly back to his office.

Melanie Clifford, Hennessey read, could offer no explanation for the rifle being in the boot of her car, nor could she offer an explanation as to how it came into her possession. Her fingerprints, in fairness, were nowhere to be found on the weapon, though neither were anybody else's. It had, like Cornelius Weekes' motor car, been wiped clean. That, in essence, was the case against Melanie Clifford. Very circumstantial in Hennessey's view, but the jury was convinced, and the bench of Appellate Court Judges were not moved to overturn the original verdict.

Hennessey studied the photograph in the file, black and white, matt, grainy and printed on coarse grained paper. The crime scene, judging by the photograph, was a rambling Victorian farmhouse, which looked like a cold building, squatting it seemed, on the naked January landscape. The victim herself was casually dressed for indoors, not outdoors, and there Hennessey noted a point which was to be added to the 'innocent' pile. How, he thought, was it possible for Melanie Clifford, rifle in hand – not a concealable handgun, but a rifle – to enter the Erickson household? Clearly a point to be addressed at some later stage, should the investigation continue its present path.

He pondered the photograph of the fatal injury, a single bullet wound to the head, to the middle of the forehead. As neatly placed as any fatal shot Hennessey had seen, though being a British police officer, gunshot wounds were not one of his greatest areas of expertise. Then, Hennessey picked up a photograph which made his blood run cold, and made his heart miss a beat. It was a photograph of Charlotte Erickson's body as it lay in the shrubbery and showed disturbance to the soil and plants caused by her lifeless body being dragged to where it was found. Plain to see were the twin tracks in the soil caused by her heels as they scoured the damp soil, but plain also were the footprints of the person who had dragged her. Two clear prints, one on either side of the body: large-sized shoes, industrial footwear, probably men's work-boots. Not the size a woman who stands at five feet nothing in her socks would be likely to have, and not the footwear of a woman suddenly summoned from her home one January evening.

Hennessey put the file down and slowly put his hand up to his mouth and wiped his lips, and gazed desperately at the corner of the room, at the Police Mutual calendar, and out of his window at a group of excited-looking Japanese tourists on the walls. Anywhere, anywhere, but the photograph. He stood, rose from his desk and made a second mug of coffee. He didn't want or need a second cup, but he desperately wanted something to do with his hands, something practical.

The implication of the two footprints was enormous. The implication that the two footprints had not been seen, or worse, ignored, was terrifying. He poured boiling water over the coffee granules, doing anything to take him away from the file of Charlotte Erickson's murder, and the dreadful realisation that was dawning on him.

He glanced out of his office window again, this time to see a party of olive-skinned youngsters all in matching red baseball caps, walking the walls, clearly following the Japanese holiday-makers; but more calmly so, more sedately. The orientals were tourists, with pressure off them for a week or two, the olive-skinned youngsters were students, Hennessey felt, from Italy or Greece, and not knowing what was ahead of them in the adult world of work and parenthood. He continued to look out of the window, very reluctant to have to return to the file which lay on his desk. But eventually he did so, with no little trepidation.

The murder of Charlotte Erickson, he noted, had taken place in the days prior to the introduction of the Police and Criminal Evidence Act. There were days when suspects could be held far longer without being charged, where a solicitor was only present upon the request of a suspect and where such a request was always interpreted as a sign of guilt, and always known by a suspect to be thus interpreted, where interviews were not recorded and crucially, where all evidence did not have to be shared with the defence lawyers. And there in the file was a photograph which pointed to a male – possibly a large, well-built male – being involved in the murder of Charlotte Erickson. At the very least, it indicated that Melanie Clifford had a male accomplice. At the most, it provided evidence to render her conviction unsafe. And it had been clearly withheld from the defence lawyers.

George Hennessey, despairing, and getting more and more dispirited by the minute saw two things: he saw a side to the up-until-then revered – and now retired – Chief Inspector John Cross, that he had not seen before, and a side he cared not for, and he also saw why Cornelius Weekes had had an interest in Melanie Clifford's conviction. Further, he thought, if, Melanie Clifford was innocent and, if her continued imprisonment suited some person or persons yet unknown, then he also saw a clear motive for Weekes' murder. So, he reasoned, the case of Melanie Clifford, and Weekes' interest in it, was probably linked to his murder after all.

Hennessey continued to read, knowing that he would find

something he didn't want to find, but that he would none-theless find it – which he did. He found it in the form of a mounted display of fingerprints which were not those of Melanie Clifford. The identity and the owner of the prints was not known but the latents had been lifted from the boot of Melanie Clifford's car – as if carelessly left there by whoever might have placed the rifle; as if carefully wiping his prints from the firearm itself but forgetting to wipe them from the paintwork of the car. Careless, very careless. He leaned forwards and picked up his phone and pressed the redial button.

"Collator."

"Hennessey, here."

"Yes, sir."

"Can you come or send someone to my office, please? Thanks." He replaced the phone and walked along the corridor to Yellich's office and standing on the threshold of his office and tapping on the doorframe as Yellich had done in Hennessey's office a little earlier that day he said "What's that word the Yanks use to describe someone who's been set up?"

"Set up, sir?"

"As in framed. You know, set up to take the consequences for a crime they didn't commit?"

"Oh. . ." Yellich searched his mind, his hand, holding a pen, was poised over the file of the murder of Cornelius Weekes. "Um . . ."

"You remember, Lee Harvey Oswald said he was one when he was arrested for the murder of J.F.K. 'I'm a . . . something . . . the word has gone from my mind.'"

"Oh . . . 'a patsy'," Yellich smiled.

"That's it." Hennessey nodded, turned, raising a hand in

thanks as he did so and walked back down the corridor to his office, repeating the word, 'patsy, patsy, patsy. . .'. He resumed his seat and waited for the constable that the collator would have sent to his office. The constable appeared in the form of an eager, fresh-faced cadet. Hennessey handed him the fingerprints he had extracted from the Erickson murder file. "The owner of these prints was not known eighteen years ago, but he or she may have come to our attention in the interim. Ask the collator to run a trace on them, please."

"Very good, sir." The cadet took the prints and left the room, rapidly, keen, eager to please.

Yellich drove home to his modest, neatly kept three-bedroom semi-detached house in Huntingdon. He was greeted by a warm hug from a weary looking Sara who suddenly burst into tears.

"Hard day?" he asked, a little obviously, he thought, but he had to say something.

"Why, does it show?" Sara Yellich forced a smile.

"A little."

"He's been impossible today, he's learnt new tricks. He's quiet now . . . I gave in. I know I shouldn't, but . . . I mean, I know what the people at the clinic said about being firm and holding on to the routine . . . but if I didn't let him have the television on, I don't know what I would have done."

"One day won't do any harm." Yellich held Sara as she again burst uncontrollably into tears. "And if he's as alert and pushy as that, he can go back to school tomorrow, sounds like he's well recovered." He squeezed her gently. "There's two things you can do," he said, calming her, "either go for a walk, calm your nerves, it's a lovely evening – it'll get you out of this prison for an hour or so – or you can go upstairs and lie down, you're obviously exhausted. In fact, why not do both in any order you like."

"Yes," she sniffed. "I think I'll do both. I'll lie down first, though, before I fall down, then I'll go for a stroll, let the evening cool off a bit first, still a bit warm for me."

"Fair enough." She kissed him and went upstairs.

Yellich walked into the sitting room of his home and saw his son sitting cross-legged on the floor gazing at the television screen, his eyes far too close to the screen and, he noted, as he did from time to time, that his son seemed suddenly bigger than he had seemed the last time he had seen him. He was already large for twelve, now he was larger.

"I hear you've been a bad lad."

"No, daddy." Jeremy turned and smiled. Then turned back to looking at the television screen, which fascinated him even when there was nothing but 'snow' caused by interference on the screen. And that was something else Yellich had to get used to of late: the television had replaced him and Sara as the centre of Jeremy's world. Seeing that an attempt to create dialogue with his son was futile, he walked to the bookcase and removed the dictionary and looked up the word 'wise'. "Well, I never . . ." he said to himself. "Well, well, well."

Later that evening, when Jeremy was asleep, Yellich and Sara sat holding each other, on the settee. Yellich said "Did you know the word 'wise' has two meanings, as well as 'wise' in the sense of being wordly wise, wise owl . . . it also means—"

"Way of doing things." Sara held up his hand and kissed it. "It was discovered in this wise—"

"It's news to me. I heard it used in the second way for

the first time today. The skipper seemed to understand, I just kept quiet and pretended that I also knew."

"What was said?"

"A woman talked about the 'wise' of her boyfriend." Yellich returned the kiss. "The wise of Cornelius Weekes. So she meant his way of doing things?"

"Yes, that's what she meant. Or his attitude, that sort of meaning. Are you forgetting that you dragged me cave man-like by the hair into a hole in the ground marked 'marriage disposal unit, females, for the purpose of'?" She dug him in the ribs with her elbow. "Tore me away from the glittering and glamorous world of teaching English to children who could hardly spell?"

"Hardly dragged, as I recall. And hardly any hair to drag you with in those days if I can remember your image at the time correctly. You could have been taken for a boy from behind."

"Often was. Come on, let's go up."

"I'm not tired."

"Good. I was hoping you'd say that."

Three

In which more is learned about the murder of Charlotte Erickson, more is learned about Melanie Clifford, and George Hennessey is host to the gracious reader.

TUESDAY

George Hennessey rose leisurely, feeling well nourished after a solid eight hours of sleep. He washed and dressed, went downstairs and let Oscar into the back garden. He delighted in the dog's enjoyment of the fresh early morning – the trace of dew, the sun risen – and Oscar criss-crossing the lawn as he always did first thing, as if reinforcing his territorial claim.

Hennessey shut the back door, knowing that Oscar would respond by testing the dog flap while he was still in the house, and which he did, turning with a patter of claw on the linoleum kitchen floor, and exited the house via the dog flap.

Hennessey sat at the kitchen breakfast bar, sipping coffee and savouring a bacon roll. Leaving the mug and the crumb-littered plate in the sink to be washed upon his return, he left the house, reaching for his summer jacket and straw hat as he did so, stealing himself against Oscar's barking protest at being left alone. He reversed his car out of the driveway, knowing that his mongrel was well provided for: a good fence that kept him in the vast rear garden, access to the cool interior of the house via the dog flap and, a bowl full of drinking water and good biscuits. Oscar had all he needed, except the constant companionship of George Hennessey. Hennessey drove from Easingwold to York, enjoying the summer morning in the Vale, and arrived at Micklegate Bar Police Station at eight thirty sharp.

He found a single note in his pigeonhole, from the collator, with compliments. The fingerprints that he had asked to be traced belonged to one David Piggot, presently aged thirty-six years, of 3, The Fold, Long Stanley. Attached to the note was a computer print-out of David Piggot's 'track'. Mild stuff, Hennessey noted. A few 'breaches' when in his twenties, a few drunk and disorderlies when in his mid-thirties, possibly, thought Hennessey, an indication of a period of crisis in his life, then nothing at all after that.

Hennessey walked along the CID corridor to Yellich's office, found the Detective Sergeant, in his shirt sleeves, watering the plant which sat atop his filing cabinet.

"Where's Long Stanley, Yellich? Do you know? And it's a place, not a person."

Yellich smiled. "Never saw it as being a fella's name before. It's out by Malton way. This side of Malton, but nearer Malton than York."

"That little town is beginning to figure large in this case."

"Is it in connection with the Erickson murder?"

"It is."

"Well, Long Stanley . . . aye . . . it belongs to Thornton le Clay and Huttons Ambo and other pleasant little villages

in that area, Whickham being another. Not a bad place –
a pub or two, a village pond, church with a square tower
and a bit of a nationalist vicar . . . always has the flag of
St George hoisted on the flagpole."

"Do you know an address called 'The Fold'?"

"Confess, I don't."

"Dare say we can always ask at the post office."

"We can, skipper?"

"We can. Grab your hat and coat, we'll take your car."

Yellich took the Malton Road out to York. Hennessey let
him clear the built up area and then broke the silence. "I'm
beginning to see a way forward with the Cornelius Weekes
murder."

"Following the trail that he followed, skipper? With
respect to the Erickson case?"

"Yes, as we are doing, but what I mean is that I think it's
going to be profitable. I now think that the Erickson case
is linked to Weekes' murder. You see, yesterday I was
looking at the Erickson file and I came across a couple of
things which to my mind question the safety of the Melanie
Clifford's conviction."

"Oh – after eighteen years. That's solemn, skipper. That's
very solemn."

"Well it could be, early days yet. She may still be
guilty, but there's a couple of things that seem to have
been conveniently ignored by the prosecution, like a male
footprint made as the body was dragged into the bushes."

"A male?"

"As I said, and the paw prints on Melanie Clifford's car.
They were checked at the time, they got that bit right, not
known, so that was that, but they looked male, too large to
be female."

"A male accomplice, skipper? Someone she's keeping quiet about?"

"Well that's one possibility that occurred to me. Yesterday I asked the collator to re-check the prints. A lot of Ouse has flowed under Lendal Bridge since those prints were lifted. Plenty of time for the owner of the prints to have had his collar felt for some misdemeanour or another."

"And he has, hence the drive to Long Stanley?"

"Correct. We're on our way to see one David Piggot, whose fingerprints were on Melanie Clifford's car. He would have been a lad of eighteen at the time. Has a strange track record. After the murder of Charlotte Erickson he got lifted for drunk and disorderly offences, then calmed down. Nothing for ten years plus, then another series of D and Ds when in his early thirties, nothing for a few years since then. Last conviction was at York Magistrates Court about two years ago. Could be nothing, could be something, but his prints were on the boot of Melanie Clifford's car, at the rim, near the lock, where the boot would be held if it was being held up to allow an item to be placed in the boot."

"An item such as a rifle, wiped clean of prints – the murder weapon used to kill Charlotte Erickson?"

"Exactly, Yellich. Exactly. So we'll see what David Piggot can tell us."

"It sounds like he's got some explaining to do, right enough. His past is casting a long shadow."

The Fold at Long Stanley was, they found, easily located by following the chirrupy voiced directions of the postmistress and revealed itself to be a cul-de-sac of council houses which was tucked away behind what was, in Hennessey's view, a magnificent stand of horse chesnuts. This was rural North Yorkshire, wealthy 'old money', farming country of picture postcard beauty, but the social mores were parochial and feudal. Council development for the least well off is broken up into small pockets and 'hidden'; at least that was what Chief Inspector Hennessey thought, who observed the area with all the advantage of having a stranger's eye.

Number three, The Fold, was the right-hand facing address of a semi-detached property. The garden was overgrown, the house seemed to have no curtains, bits of rusting components from motor cars littered the driveway. Hennessey and Yellich walked up the drive, aware of curtains twitching in adjacent houses, as they wound their way between engine blocks, or stepped over rear axles. They walked past the front of the house, and its front door, and instead walked to the door at the side of the house which, they knew, was the most regularly used point of egress and entry in such houses.

Hennessey knocked on the door causing a large dog to bark excitedly. The echoing quality of the bark said much to Hennessey about the state of furnishing and decoration in the house: loudly echoing, spartanly furnished. The door opened to reveal a large-boned woman with a red face and matted silver hair, who could have been anywhere from thirty to fifty. She had a hot searing breath and bleary eyes. She held a meaty hand round a thick leather metal studded collar which itself was fastened round the neck of a snarling Alsation crossbreed.

"Police?" the woman asked but didn't display any animosity. In fact both Hennessey and Yellich found her manner deferential and humble.

"Yes, afraid so." Hennessey showed his ID. Yellich reached for his, but the woman shook her head and said that if one was genuine, the other would be too. "We're looking for a David Piggot," Hennessey explained. "We have this on file as his last known address." The woman's face creased and she looked to the officers to be close to tears.

"Aye, this was his last known address . . . his last ever address . . . he died about two years ago, aye . . . two years this summer."

"Oh . . . I'm sorry. You are?"

"His wife . . . well not really. I suppose I'm nothing really." She tugged the dog back beside her. "We were common-law, never married proper, so I'm either his widow or I'm not, depending. Pauline's my name."

"I see, Pauline. Could we ask you some questions? It's probably nothing for you to worry about."

"Aye," she smiled. "The last time the police said that to me I was arrested for shoplifting. I'll just put Jasper in the hall." She retreated, pulling the dog with her. The officers heard the opening and closing of internal doors and then the woman returned to the threshold of the side door of her home. "Come in." She turned and the officers followed her inside. The house, while pleasantly cool inside was also untidy, stale aired and sticky surfaced. It was not the sort of house either Yellich or Hennessey would feel comfortable sitting down in, especially in an upholstered chair.

"Sit down." The woman collapsed backwards into an armchair.

"We'll stand if you don't mind," Hennessey smiled.

"Suit yourself. Mind I don't blame you, between me and the dog, I'm probably in the driest chair. I never said it was Buckingham Palace. So you're after our Davy . . . well, like I said he's gone where you can't catch him."

"What happened?" Hennessey asked. "An accident? Thirty plus is a bit young for natural causes . . . I mean not unknown by any means, but a bit young."

"Accident . . . he was drinking, fell in front of a lorry in Piccadilly, the Piccadilly in York, not London. He'd gone into York for a good session."

"I see." Hennessey glanced out of the rear window at the washing on the line, which was strung diagonally over a long grassed rear lawn. So tall was the grass that the lower edges of the washing hung below the top of the grass.

"He'd been drinking lately, I mean just before he died."

"We noticed that," Hennessey said. "Going by his record, some disorderly offences when he was a youngster, then nothing until he was in his thirties."

"He'd calmed down like all hotheads do. That is if they don't kill themselves first. When I met him he wasn't drinking, he was a good, steady worker. Farmhand, jobbing gardener for folk, especially the old folk. Lots of them can't manage their gardens any more. Last thing he turned his hand to was trying to make money dealing in cars . . . it wasn't a good idea."

"We noticed the bits on the drive."

"That's Davy, that's Davy's bits. I've got used to them now. I'll miss them if the council take them away. Davy could take cars apart but he had trouble putting them back together again. He should have stuck to gardening. He was going to go back to it. Then he fell under a lorry."

"Did Davy ever tell you about his involvement in anything a bit more serious than being drunk and disorderly?"

The woman paused, looked at Hennessey, the older, wiser-looking one, then at Yellich, the more youthful one, then at Hennessey again and said, "So you know about that?"

"Yes," Hennessey nodded, pleased that Yellich was composed enough not to glance at him. That would have given the game away. "Yes we know, and we'd like to know what you know."

"I wasn't involved."

"We know that."

"I met him after it."

"When he was sober and calm?"

"Aye . . . a good, steady worker. I did well to find him. So I thought." She smiled self-effacingly. "Not left me with much has he? So what can I tell you."

"Just what you know. In your own words. See if it checks out with what we know."

"Well, he was sober for ten years, just a few beers at the weekend up the Three Magpies on Friday and Saturday nights with the other guys from the estate. Then one Friday he comes home early, well before last orders, and he's really pale, really shaken, he said it wasn't true what they say, you don't drink to forget, he said you drink to remember. He just kept himself to himself all that weekend, but looking . . . well looking like he was on another planet. Later he told me that he'd remembered something when he was drinking, a memory had come flooding back, and then it had taken him two more days to work out whether he was remembering a dream or whether it was real. Eventually he decided that it was real because he could remember the smells."

"What did he remember doing?"

"Putting something in the boot of a car. He didn't say what, and he said he was careful not to get his prints on whatever it was he put in the boot of the car, but when it was too late he realised that he'd taken his glove off so as to be able to turn the key in the lock. He couldn't get a proper grip of the key with thick working gloves. He said he must have left his prints all over the car. Some time went by, about a year, and then he got arrested for the first time. The police took his prints but by then someone had been arrested and gaoled for some crime or other, and so his prints weren't matched to any outstanding crimes. He got drunk a few more times then he got into his sober period. But a few years ago, he was drinking in the Magpies and it all came flooding back – so he said. He said it didn't come all at once, but different bits at different times and not in the right order. He said it took him week to remember all the bits and put them in the right order."

"Did he tell you any details?" The woman shook her head. "He didn't. Just that he had to wait for a car to pull up, wait for the driver to get out, wait for her—"

"Her?"

"Yes, the driver was a woman. Wait for her to get out and leave the car, walk away, then put whatever it was he had to put in the car – in the car – and make himself scarce, his job was done then."

"That's all?"

"Well that's all he told me."

"But he had keys to the car?"

"So he said."

"Why did he do it?"

"He didn't say. I assume it was for money. He was a young lad, wanted his beer money. But he didn't seem to know the woman. Had to have the car described to him, he said – he had to wait for a white Vauxhall. But it was more than remembering what he did, it was also as if he realised something else even worse. He realised that someone was innocent, a female, he said, 'She's innocent', and it was that that set him off in the wrong direction. He started to drink again, and I mean drink, and eventually fell under a lorry.

67

There was an inquest: the lorry driver said that Davy seemed to be watching the lorry approach and he seemed to stagger into it, under its wheels."

"Suicide?"

"The verdict was misadventure. He didn't launch himself under the wheels, wasn't as clear as that, but the lorry driver said that he had the strong impression that Davy was ending it all. He said that Davy wasn't so out of control that he couldn't have saved himself. That's what the lorry driver said."

"I see." Hennessey paused. "Now . . . the location that Davy put the item in the car?"

"Never said where it was."

"Do you know who he was working for at the time?"

"Erickson. He employs a few folk round here. Davy said that he was working for Erickson from the day he left school to just before he met me, about five years with Erickson. And he did what he did before he met me. So he was working for Erickson at the time."

"Thank you, Miss—"

"Bailey," the woman smiled. "I've gone back to my maiden name. Was that some help?"

"Yes. Thank you. It was very useful, it confirmed a lot," Hennessey smiled.

"Aye – only you couldn't see your way to helping me out? I don't get my welfare money 'til Thursday and Jasper through there, well he's a big dog and he needs his feed." Hennessey took out his wallet and put a few notes of paper money on the sticky surface of the sideboard.

"Generous, skipper," Yellich said as he drove away from The Fold and Long Stanley, back towards York.

"That sort of gesture, – Yellich, let me tell you, – that

68

sort of gesture is what makes the world go round. You'll realise that, especially when your own retirement appears on your horizon. When that happens, the realisation dawns on you that you're soon never to be visiting households like that again."

"Even so, skipper, especially since what you gave her will buy stuff to go down her own neck, not Jasper's."

"The information was good, Yellich. It moves us on, and it moves us on muchly." Hennessey glanced out of the car window, and savoured the Vale in May time: the foliage, the newness, the warmth, the promise of summer to come, and the wide landscape of greens and yellows under a vast blue sky. "It's getting to be clear what it was that Cornelius Weekes was driving at. It's a pity for him that his 'wise', as his girlfriend poetically called it, was also to worry."

"Worry, skipper? About what?"

"No. I mean worry, as in worry at something, to harass, to persist . . ."

"I didn't know—" But Yellich's voice trailed off as he realised that DC Hennessey was deep in thought.

Yellich and Hennessey sat opposite each other in the canteen that lunchtime. The room also served as the police bar and at one thirty p.m. the grill of the bar was raised noisily in anticipation of officers on the six-'til-two shift wanting an after-work beer. Or two.

"Should have gone out." Hennessey prodded the meat pie and pondered the soggy chips. Then he pushed the plate away from him. "Up with this, I shall not put. Should have gone out, I can afford it. Should have gone out."

"I've noticed that you do that, skipper, go out to eat at lunchtime." Yellich cut a piece from his fried haddock and prodded it with his fork. "I mean, all right, this is real school meals, but it's cheap, and if you remember that two-thirds of the world is going hungry, then this can taste quite nice, really."

"Well that's the right attitude, I suppose, unless of course you're building up a resistance to the essential awkwardness of canteen grub. Or just getting used to it, or whatever."

"Probably, but a three-course meal for less than a pint in your local, that's not bad, even if it is tasteless and lukewarm."

"It's not even lukewarm. I ate in here today because I thought I'd been indulging myself with too many lunches out. Now I believe I was being sensible. I'm going to feel irritated for the rest of the day now. And getting out for an hour is good, helps clarify your thoughts."

"Speaking of the rest of the day, skipper, what's on?"

"Aside from the mountain of work to do in the Weekes case, you mean?"

"Well, I was thinking particularly about the Weekes case, skipper."

"Cross-refer the Weekes and Erickson cases to each other, will you? They're linking strongly now. Do that as soon as after lunch. I'm as certain as I can be that Cornelius was burrowing away at Melanie Clifford's wrongful conviction."

"As good as done, skipper. So they're cross-referenced – what then? Visit Melanie Clifford?"

"Not yet. Can you confirm that she's definitely in Durham? And I want to find out more about her. This afternoon we're going our separate ways."

"We are?"

"We are."

"I want to go to York City, access the archives and pick Dr D'Acre's brains about the post-mortem findings in Charlotte Erickson's murder. I'd like you to visit Melanie Clifford's sister."

"I didn't know she had one."

"She may not still, eighteen years is a long time and many people have met their maker in the last eighteen years – at least one person relevant to this inquiry has as we found this morning. But eighteen years ago Melanie Clifford gave her sister's name as being her next of kin. I remember catching sight of it on the front sheet of her file. Chase her up, will you? Get a measure of Melanie as a person – as much as you can. If I don't see you back here before close of play today, we'll compare notes first thing tomorrow."

"Very good, skipper." Yellich finished his fish and chips and then turned to his apple pie and custard.

Hennessey put his half-eaten main meal and his untouched pudding on his tray. Then he paused and asked Yellich if he could 'rescue' his dessert. Yellich raised a keen eyebrow and mumbled 'thanks', and rescued the pudding from Hennessey, who then carried his tray to the self-clear area and left the canteen feeling short-changed.

Hennessey knew that he should walk. The journey was really no distance at all, even for a man in his late middle years. Micklegate Bar Police Station to York District Hospital? A mile. If that. And most of the walk would the walker through the fascinating medieval centre of York. It could be fun, too, first walking the walls and then descending to street level to explore a path through the snickelways, the myriad small passages that weave through the urban fabric of the city, like a street system within a street system.

But it was a hot day. He was uncomfortable in the heat, especially in the city, and so he drove, windows down, fan full on, and found that he regretted this indulgence. The engine of his car had only just warmed when he reached his destination. He turned into the car park of the hospital and parked at the first convenient space. He walked across the car park and, as he did so, he scanned the expanse of tarmac and gleaming multi-coloured metal of Dr D'Acre's car, and smiled when he saw it – the Riley, red and white. It was parked in the 'Doctors Only' space in the car park.

Hennessey entered the medium-rise slab-sided building and followed the signs to the Pathology Department. He located Louise D'Acre where he knew he'd find her, in her small study adjacent to the post-mortem theatre. She glanced up at him and welcomed him with a smile which said 'hello' but it also said 'role only – keep your distance'.

"Dr D'Acre." Hennessey took off his hat. "I have a favour to ask." She raised her eyebrows but her face was expressionless, utterly focused on her work.

"A murder was committed eighteen years ago, in the York area. There would have been a post-mortem most probably done in this hospital. Would the records still be here?"

"Yes. We keep our P-M records for twenty years, then they get sent to central records where they are kept indefinitely, placed on microfiche perhaps, but kept nonetheless. So if the record you wish to access has been sent up early for space-saving reasons, you'll still be able to access it. So, one way or another, you be able to access the file you want. Do you have a name?"

"Charlotte Erickson." He sat, invited, in the vacant chair.

"Nice name, rather classy."

"It is, isn't it. Sadly, it didn't save her from an untimely death. Just twenty-seven years old when she was shot."

"Twenty-seven . . ." Louise D'Acre repeated as she pressed a four-figure number on her phone. "Yes, pathology here, Dr D'Acre. I'd like access to a file, a forensic pathology report – a Charlotte Erickson . . . twenty-seven . . . about eighteen years ago. Yes, as soon as possible, please . . . thanks." She replaced the phone and turned to Hennessey. "Shot, you say?"

"In the head."

"Why the interest now?"

"Well," Hennessey relaxed in his chair. "It is possible, in fact highly probable, that her murder links up to the murder of the young man found in his fume-filled car on Sunday morning."

"The suicide that never was – that's interesting."

"It's interesting in a chilling sort of way. You see, it's possible that the wrong person was convicted of the murder of Charlotte Erickson, and that person remains to this day in prison."

"Oh . . ." Louise D'Acre looked genuinely distressed.

"It's a huge chunk out of anybody's life – about a quarter of a reasonable life span – and if she was innocent all along . . . well, it's not going to be a good day for the police force."

There was a gentle, deferential tap on the open door of Louise D'Acre's office. A young, bespectacled woman stood at the entrance to the office holding a file in her hands. Dr D'Acre stood and held out her hand for the file saying, "Thank you, Janet, that was quick." Hennessey liked her for that. He liked her for standing and smiling and saying thank you and adding a compliment. Other members of a senior profession would have leaned back imperiously and let 'Janet', who had clearly recently left school, place the file on the desk in front of them.

Dr D'Acre resumed her seat and opened the file.

"Ah . . ." she said more to herself than to Hennessey. "Tom Hext performed this P-M. One of the last he did before he retired, it would seem. He was a respected man, not one of the greats of his era, no Spilsbury here. He didn't add to the body of professional knowledge, but a solid and dependable pathologist. He was good enough, though, for any police force or Coroners' Court who had his service to count themselves lucky."

"Well, to come from you that's an accolade indeed."

"So, what can I tell you?"

"The nuts and bolts of the murder"

"The nuts and bolts . . ." Louise D'Acre scanned the file. "The nuts and bolts are simply that she was shot in the head. She was shot by a small calibre weapon – a .22 – the entry wound was the middle of her forehead and had a flat trajectory." Louise D'Acre held a ballpoint pen at ninety degrees to her forehead, "It entered at that sort of angle. Assuming that the victim, Charlotte Erickson was standing when she was shot, the bullet would have travelled a path roughly parallel to the ground." She scanned further. "I see the victim was found out of doors and it's a truism to say that most people who are murdered out of doors are on their feet in one way or another. People who are murdered when sitting, or prostrate, are most often murdered indoors. Plentiful exceptions to prove the rule but, as a generalisation, it's acceptable, and I note the murder took place in the January of that year, not a time when folk would lie down and sunbathe or laze in deckchairs."

"You're clouding and clearing the issue."

"How?" Louise D'Acre spoke sternly. "Clouding and clearing are mutually exclusive."

"What I mean is, that you are clarifying my thoughts that Melanie Clifford is innocent. But you are presenting me with a cloudy mystery in its place. You see, the person convicted of the murder is only five feet tall."

"Ah . . ." Louise D'Acre turned the front sheet of the file. "Charlotte Erickson was five feet eight inches tall. I see your concern. Have you visited the murder scene?"

"No. I've seen photographs but have not visited."

"Is it flat?"

"Appears to be . . . flat level ground outside a large house."

"No local variation in ground elevation – like a landscaped golf course, for example."

"It doesn't appear that way. Why?"

"Well, if the victim and the perpetrator were both standing, and the ground was level, then the perpetrator would have to be sufficiently tall, that his shoulder was the same height as the victim's forehead. He, or she, would have been, well, over six feet tall. That's the only way the flat trajectory could have been achieved. If . . . what was her name?"

"Melanie Clifford."

"Yes. If she was the murderer then she would have had to be standing on a wooden box in order to shoot a bullet into Charlotte Erickson's forehead with a flat trajectory. If she was standing on the ground, the bullet would have entered Charlotte Erickson's forehead with an inclined trajectory . . . so." Dr D'Acre placed the ballpoint against her head at about twenty degrees from the horizontal. "Perhaps not so steep, but a definite upward trajectory. The only other explanation is that she was shot from some distance away, a few hundred yards – thus influenced by wider ground elevation. I'm not a ballistics expert, but I have always thought a .22 was a close range weapon."

"It is. Even a rifle is designed for shooting vermin in the confines of a farmyard."

"I'm surprised at Tom Hext . . . but perhaps not – he simply reported his findings. Who was the investigating police officer?"

"Fellow called John Cross – similarly to Tom Hext, also now retired and this was one of his last cases. I remember him. I had a lot of time for him."

"Had?"

"Well, missing the issue of the trajectory of the bullet, and one or two other points: male footprints round the corpse and male paw prints on the car in which the murder weapon was found. We identified the owner, now no longer with us. He as good as confessed to his partner that he placed the murder weapon in the car, but that is not admissible in evidence. I don't think – I can't believe in my heart of hearts, that John Cross wilfully withheld or ignored information which pointed to Melanie Clifford's innocence. But I am beginning to wonder whether or not he had a degree of 'tunnel vision' thinking on this one. I mean, so convinced was he of Melanie Clifford's guilt that without realising it, he unknowingly, unconsciously closed his mind to any indication of her innocence."

"That's not an unknown attitude. Sadly. And this, of course, was pre-P.A.C.E. days."

"That thought was crossing my mind," Hennessey sighed. "John Cross could be a bit of a tyrant, especially if he thought someone was guilty. I shudder to think of him interviewing

Melanie Clifford, arm up her back, figuratively, if not literally. I confess that now I'm beginning to wonder about his other 'successes'."

"Well, that's for you to take further – the time of death was uncertain. Tom Hext would only commit himself to a wide envelope of up to forty-eight hours – the winter conditions, you see, arrested the rate of decomposition."

"Forty-eight hours?" Hennessey's hand went up to his forehead. "The prosecution alleged that she was shot the evening before Melanie Clifford was arrested, thus implying that the murder had taken place six or seven hours earlier – now you tell me the woman could have been dead for up to two days before she was found. And John Cross knew that!"

"Yes . . . please don't shout at me. It's not my fault."

Hennessey paused. "Sorry."

"The time of death is difficult to determine. We are not very good at it. Cause yes, but time . . . that's a different matter. If someone was seen alive at ten p.m. and found dead at six a.m., then you'd know they died some time between ten p.m. and six a.m. and, frankly, forensic pathology couldn't pin the t.o.d. down tighter than that. Too, too, many variables. Come to me for cause, but I'll take a rain-check on time. She could have been murdered the evening before she was found, the forty-eight hours is merely Tom Hext covering himself. He says 'up to forty-eight hours', not 'about forty-eight hours'."

"And the defence counsel, what were they playing at?" Again Hennessey's hand went up to his forehead. "I'm already able to drive a coach and six through John Cross's case and I have no paper qualifications at all, let alone Law Society exams."

"And she's still inside?" Louise D'Acre closed the file.

"Yes, as I said, she collected life – that was mandatory – but the judge who was clearly of the 'hanging fraternity', recommended that she serve a minimum of twenty years. I remember the case, and at the time I had little sympathy for her."

"And now?"

"Now . . . the whole affair is beginning to make me ashamed of being a police officer."

"Don't take it personally," the man smiled. Yellich viewed him as being a little overweight. But not so seriously, given his age, baldness, stainless-steel spectacles, warm face, round eyes, and what seemed a genuine smile.

"I don't. You rapidly develop a thick skin and a broad back once you join the police force."

"I can well imagine. But I believe I'll be able to answer all your questions."

They sat in the living room of a modest house in Dringhouses. There were photographs of young people in university gowns, proudly holding degree certificates which Yellich believed spoke of proud parents or grandparents. Probably the latter, Yellich thought, estimating the man in whose house he was sitting to be in his sixties.

"So why the interest, now, after all this time?"

"It follows the murder of the newspaper man."

"Oh . . . you know I feared as much . . . oh yes . . . Mr Weekes . . . nice young man, very pleasant . . . we read all about his murder in the *Post*, made to look like suicide . . . but we didn't connect it with Melanie's situation . . . not at first, but I did wonder if he rattled the wrong cage."

"Mr Weekes visited you?"

"Oh yes, quite recently, asking questions about Melanie. Now my wife was quite ready and in fact eager to speak to him – I'm afraid it's the police she harbours a feeling of black hatred for. She doesn't distinguish one police officer from another – each and every police officer is a focus for her hatred. But Mr Weekes, well, he seemed to be on our side, as it were."

"We don't take sides as such, Mr Burnett, save for seeking to convict the guilty and protect the innocent."

"And sometimes you get it wrong."

"Sometimes," Yellich conceded. "How did Mr Weekes come to hear of your sister-in-law's situation?"

"My wife contacted him. Read his name in the paper and wrote to him asking for his help. She actually wrote to a lot of people in the media but few showed any interest. So tell me, Mr Yellich . . . sorry, that was your name?"

"Yellich, yes, Detective Sergeant."

"So what position are you in? Are you interested in the murder of Cornelius Weekes, or are you finally prepared to look at the circus that was the conviction of my sister-in-law, and which was damn near the ruination of my wife's health. It's something that the police don't seem to realise: when someone from a good family is convicted, the entire family pay a penalty. It's only by a fortitude, which I didn't know my wife possessed, that she has managed to hang on to her sanity. So what's your motivation here?"

"Justice, Mr Burnett. Simply that. Justice. Mr Weekes' murder is leading us to look again at the murder of Charlotte Erickson."

A silence. Heavy. Pregnant. A car drove past in the road outside the front window, beyond the small front garden.

"I am barely containing my anger, Mr Yellich." Mr

Burnett looked down at the carpet, a busy pattern on a black background. "I tell you, it's going to be a bad day for the police when this is made public. It appears that it takes the murder of a young man before you are prepared to reinvestigate the most unsafe of all unsafe convictions."

"The Crown had a strong argument – a scorned woman, the murder weapon in her car—"

"But you see it falls apart already, Melanie was not a scorned woman. She wasn't. It's difficult to explain. Melanie and Toby Erickson had an odd sort of relationship. They kept going off and on each other over a period of about ten years, and their 'off' periods could be as long as eighteen months, during which one or the other or both sometimes took up with someone else, with the knowledge and approval of the other. Then should they get to talking at a time when neither was involved with any other person, they'd go into one of their 'on' periods for a few months. And they saw a lot of each other because Melanie was employed by Toby."

"I didn't know that."

"Oh yes . . . in a secretarial, clerical capacity and, anyway, when Toby and Charlotte met it was during one of Melanie and Toby's 'off' periods. They had been 'off' each other for a few months by then. So he didn't leave her for Charlotte. When Toby and Charlotte announced their engagement, Melanie sent them a congratulations card and bought a gift for their wedding, though she didn't attend the ceremony as such, it wouldn't have been seemly. So does that sound like a scorned woman?"

Yellich remained silent. He wouldn't be drawn.

Burnett continued, an icy, hard edge creeping into his voice, as though he had been infected with his wife's hatred. "There's also the lack of logic in the Crown's argument.

If Melanie was removing a 'love' rival from the scene, wouldn't she do it before the wedding, not afterwards? Wouldn't that make more sense?"

"Possibly."

"Probably, I'd say – and with a very high degree of probability at that. And the murder weapon itself . . . a rifle. Have you met Melanie?"

"No."

"She's tiny. She's a very small woman, very finely made, she hasn't got the strength to lift a rifle, hold a steady arm and squeeze the trigger. And if the thing was found in her car, well, so what? It's the easiest thing in the world, to plant evidence. She drove a popular make of car, any random bunch of car keys would contain a key that would open the boot."

"The drive to Erickson's house, late one January night – what's the explanation for that?"

"I believe . . . we believe that Melanie retained contact with Toby and became a friend of the family after the marriage and if he were to phone and say, 'Look, sorry, I know it's late but we've got a problem, can you possibly come over right now?' well, knowing Melanie, she'd oblige him. She probably wouldn't be pleased, but she'd go, she'd pull her socks on and go."

"But Toby Erickson wasn't at home."

"So it seemed. We know that now. But he wouldn't have had to be at home." Burnett forced a smile and pointed to a red phone beside his chair which to Yellich's taste jarred with the colour scheme of the room, and did so violently. "I can phone my brother in Australia from here. Toby could have phoned Melanie from anywhere in the world and asked her to join him at Coles Copse

Farm. She wouldn't have known where he was phoning from."

"You seem to be pointing an accusing finger at Toby Erickson?"

"Mr Yellich, let me make it plain to you that my wife and I have never pointed an accusing finger at anyone, we have been very careful about that. Throughout, we have pointed only to the lack of safety of Melanie's conviction. In fact, we have done more than that, we have pointed to her innocence." Burnett paused. "Though, having said that, I do concede that when it comes to the issue of Toby Erickson's involvement, both my wife and I have harboured certain suspicions, but we have kept them to ourselves. They have not been voiced."

"I see . . . and Mr Weekes, did he voice suspicion?"

"He didn't say. But, back to Melanie. You know she's not a murder personality. I am recently retired from the library service but, since Melanie's conviction, I used quiet periods in the library to do a lot of reading and I became a bit of a para-criminologist, and I have read learned texts about matters forensic and there is, by all accounts, an identifiable murder personality: a low flash point, a frighteningly self-orientated 'the sun shines just for me' attitude, a dislike of living things, neglectful of plants and ill-treatment of pets, for example. Such is the murder personality, and that apparently includes the so-called crimes of passion, as well as the cold-blooded, premeditated murderers. But Melanie was none of those things . . . her small house was full of thriving, healthy plants, and when she was arrested all she was concerned about was the welfare of her animals; a cat and a dog. In fact she made the one phone call she was allowed to make to phone my wife, her sister, to ask her to look after the pets and water the plants."

"She didn't ask for a solicitor?"

"No. I think she assumed that she wouldn't need one. She stuck to her story which the police clearly thought to be too outlandish to be true, and she was devastated when she was charged, but she, and we, remained confident about the outcome of the trial. We had faith in the British criminal justice system. She – and we – didn't fully realise that once you are charged, you seem to begin a long slide downwards, gathering momentum as you go and, the further you slide down, the more difficult it is to stop the slide and escape the system. I dare say the trick is not to step on the slide in the first place, but we don't believe she did step on the slide. We believe she was pushed on to it."

Burnett paused, as if absorbing some difficult emotion, then he continued. "But whether she stepped on to it of her own volition, or whether she was pushed, the fact remains that she was on the slide and down she went. We attended the trial, of course, all three days of it, and I believe I can recover in my memory every word that was spoken. It's an ominous building, the York Crown Court building. She was not best served by the barrister . . . a young man who I didn't think was destined to go far at the Bar. He seemed a bit emotionally immature and a little out of his depth. Rather than fighting Melanie's corner, he seemed to be trying to win the case by smiling appeasing smiles at the judge. I have often wondered whether his performance contributed to the 'twenty year minimum' recommendation that the judge handed down as part of the life sentence. He was a sour old soul, the judge. I had the impression that he'd be capable of doing that, the twenty year minimum I mean, doing that to transmit a message to Melanie's barrister that trials cannot be won by that sort of coercion. It was a reasonable message to transmit to the man, but not at the expense of his client. That's my view.

"You know who you should talk to? Charlotte's family. I'll let you have their address. They were at the trial. And after it, her father approached us and said that even though it was his daughter who had been murdered, and even though he thirsted for justice, neither he nor his wife were convinced that the police had charged the right person. Cornelius said that he was going to call them and request an interview.

"I'll just get their address and phone number for you, but I can tell you now you'll have to mind your 'p's and 'q's. They're country set, very old money, and large quantities of it." He crossed the room and opened the desk top of a darkly stained bureau which stood against the wall and from within the bureau he removed a small leather-bound notebook. He turned the pages. "Yes, here it is . . . Ffrench – two f's – I told you they were old money and the Ffrenches all live happily—"

"Happily?"

"Sorry, I was being facetious . . . they live at The Dower House, Long Stanley."

"Long Stanley!"

"Yes. It's a village near Malton. Is that significant?"

"Probably. It's just that me and my boss had occasion to go there just this morning."

"In connection with Melanie's case?"

"Well . . . yes."

"In what way connected?"

"I can't tell you."

"I see." Burnett replaced the notebook and closed the

bureau. He remained standing. "There's something you should know about Melanie – you'll be visiting her doubtless, so you should know."

"What?"

"She's blind."

"Blind?"

"Yes, no identifiable cause – no injury, no disease – so the medics have put it down to hysterical blindness. It's her reaction to the much-vaunted world famous criminal justice system which she, and we, feel failed her so dismally, so dreadfully. The appeal was a re-hash of the original trial and she woke up the day after her appeal failed to find that she had gone blind. So not only has she spent the last eighteen years in prison for a crime that we firmly believe she didn't commit, but she's spent fifteen of those eighteen years in complete darkness. Quite a penalty to pay for getting into your car one January night in order to do a favour for a friend. You may now perhaps understand why my wife refuses to speak to a police officer?"

George Hennessey returned to Micklegate Bar Police Station and wrote up his findings and observations and thoughts about the murder of Charlotte Erickson based on his discussion with Dr D'Acre in the by then reopened Erickson file. He took the Weekes file and in it he wrote 'see Erickson file for possible motive.' By five p.m. Yellich still hadn't returned from visiting the Burnett household and so he signed out and drove home.

He enjoyed that early summer evening, in the Vale of York. There was, he thought, even for a Londoner like himself, no better place to be. On his return to his detached house in Easingwold, he had been warmly welcomed by

Oscar who jumped up at him and turned in excited, very tight, tail-wagging circles. Hennessey made a pot of tea and later stood drinking it from a huge mug in the garden at the rear of his house, 'talking' to Jennifer.

When he and Jennifer, as newly-weds, had bought the house, the back garden was an unimaginative slab of green sward, a little like a cricket pitch. And when Jennifer was heavily pregnant with Charles she had sat down one day at the kitchen table and drawn plans for a more imaginative garden. The lawn, she decided, would be bordered by herbaceous flowers and split across the middle by a privet hedge, in which a gateway would be set. The 'lower lawn', being the lawn beyond the privet, would be planted with apple trees and would also contain, tucked away in a corner, a potting shed and a tool shed. The very bottom of the garden would be, she had decided – having been inspired by Francis Bacon's essay 'Of gardens' – the 'going forth' and left as waste land where it would be the home of any nature that wished to grow there, which had transpired to be coarse grass. But within the 'going forth' Jennifer had decreed that a pond be sunk and native amphibians introduced.

George Hennessey, eager to accommodate his lovely young wife's wishes had then set to, in his spare time, with spade and hoe, sprig of privet, saplings of apple tree, and two 'assemble-at-home' garden sheds, to create the garden to Jennifer's design.

It was then that tragedy had struck George Hennessey's life, and it was not the first time that it had so struck. It was just when all was going so wonderfully, when Charles – perfect in every way and who had been born of an uncomplicated and speedy delivery – was three months old and making his presence felt that Jennifer had died.

She had been walking through the centre of Easingwold on a hot summer's afternoon, carrying two shopping bags, when life had suddenly left her. She had crumpled to the pavement, folk rushed to her aid, believing her to have fainted, but no pulse was to be found and she was pronounced dead on arrival at hospital, or 'Condition Purple' in paramedic speak.

Jennifer's cause of death was given as Sudden Death Syndrome because the medical profession could not, and still cannot, explain why – without warning – a healthy young person should have their life force extracted from their body. But it happens, and it seemed to Hennessey that about every four or five years he would read of a case of SDS being reported, often meriting no more than a few column inches of local newspaper space. Yet he knew from his own experience what that small column space meant to a family. The unfairness of it, the cruelty of it, for the victims often seemed to him to be, like Jennifer, people in their twenties – the hole left behind, picking up the pieces, the carrying on, as his father said, 'carry on regardless'.

He had scattered Jennifer's ashes on her garden, a little bit here and there until he felt in some way she occupied all of it. She was in the 'going forth', she was in the pond among the amphibia, she was in the orchard, she was on the lawn, and she was also in the garden at the front of the house.

He never let a day go past without stepping into the garden, sometimes to say 'hello' to Jennifer but, more often, as on that lovely evening, to talk to her. That evening he told her about the disturbing revelation regarding Melanie Clifford's conviction but, not wanting to distress her had said, 'don't worry, dear heart, we'll get there in the end.

I know we will'. He had then returned to the house and settled down with an obscure text, a reprint of a soldier's eye view of the Peninsular War. A short piece, but simply written, the combination, he felt, of a very intelligent mind that only had access to a limited vocabulary. It was recently chanced upon in a jumble sale and instantly became a valued addition to his library of military history.

When the sun was down and the evening was cool enough not to cause discomfort to Oscar who, being a tan dog, suffered in the heat, Hennessey fed him and they took their evening walk together. One man and his dog. An observer would see them as being very happy to be in each other's company. Later, it was another walk this time just Hennessey alone, a stroll into Easingwold for a glass of stout – just the one – before last orders were called.

It was, he felt, a very enjoyable evening.

Four

In which two very contrasting lifestyles are met, and George Hennessey is visited by his son, in whom he is well pleased.

WEDNESDAY

The Dower House in Long Stanley, near Malton, was as Burnett had described. It was a generously proportioned early Victorian mansion which stood in plentiful grounds at the end of a tree-lined drive. Beyond the grounds was lush pasture in gently rolling fields, the landscape being broken up with the occasional small wood. There was, so far as Hennessey and Yellich could see, apart from the outbuildings, just one other building within perhaps a half-mile, and that was a Dutch barn. The Dower House was a building of wide frontage, one side of which was covered with Virginia creeper. A wide gravel-covered forecourt gave way to a lawn so neatly and closely cut that Hennessey thought it would be best described as 'manicured', and in the middle of which was an elaborate stone statue of a male figure in a loincloth wrestling with a serpent. Above was a wide blue sky in which the sun was perhaps one quarter of its way through its transit over North Yorkshire.

Yellich slowed the car to a halt, noisily, on the gravel close to the imposing front door of the house. He and Hennessey got out of the car and walked across the forecourt to the short flight of steps up to the front door. There was no knocker, no bell to press as there would be on a suburban house, but instead they found a metal ring, about six inches in diameter, protruding from the stonework beside the door.

"Pull it," Hennessey suggested.

Yellich did so, tugging it twice, and creating a rather pleasant jangling of many bells which echoed in the house, suggesting that the interior was both cavernous and palatial. The door was lazily opened, it seemed, and only after a full minute – a long time in such circumstances – after the sound of the echoing bells had died. A stern-faced woman stood there, in a white blouse and black skirt. She wore a solemn expression. Eventually, clearly doing things on her terms, she said, "Good morning, gentlemen, may I help you?"

"Police." Hennessey showed his ID. Yellich did the same.

"Yes, gentlemen?"

"We'd like to speak to Mr and or Mrs Ffrench."

"Concerning?"

"That's confidential."

"I see. If you'd like to step this way, gentlemen." The maid turned and led Hennessey and Yellich into the pleasantly cool interior of the house: they found vast solid tables, oil paintings hanging on the walls, crystal chandeliers, a wide staircase, angling upwards, polished wooden floors, wood-panelled walls – all beneath a ceiling painted in a pastel shade of blue. The maid opened the double doors of a drawing room and invited Hennessey and Yellich to wait in the room, then she shut the door behind her.

"Well, Mr Burnett did say it was old money," Yellich said.

"A lot of it." Hennessey looked around him. He read a cluttered room, very Victorian, the eye assaulted at every turn: stuffed birds in huge glass bell-jars, chaise longues, leather armchairs and a settee, framed oil paintings covering the wall and brown velvet curtains hanging either side of the sash windows, which looked out on to a rear lawn. Possibly, thought Hennessey, a full acre in measurement, neatly cut into contrasting strips, bounded by a wall on one side and a high hedge at the bottom and on the other side. "You mentioned that he said that as well. He seems to have been right on both counts."

Yellich looked at Hennessey. The two men held eye contact but said nothing, though each pondered the same issue: the implication of Mr Burnett, brother-in-law to Melanie Clifford, having been proved correct in respect of one of his observations.

A full ten minutes elapsed, during which Hennessey and Yellich stood in almost complete silence. Then the double doors were pulled open and a middle-aged man in T-shirt and jeans entered and beamed confidently at Hennessey and Yellich. "Police?" he asked.

"We are . . . you're Mr Ffrench?" Hennessey made no attempt to disguise his puzzlement.

"You seemed surprised? I am Mr Ffrench, Benjamin Ffrench."

"I am, I was expecting someone a little older. We are calling in connection with the murder of Charlotte Erickson."

The man's face hardened as if a raw wound had been touched. "She was my sister," he said simply. Our parents are now elderly, as you may imagine. My father has a frail heart and has to be kept free of stress and mother's mind is leaving her. I know all that they know about Charlotte's murder. You can direct any question to me. Shall we sit down? I'm sorry to have kept you waiting," Ffrench offered them leather armchairs and a settee which creaked as they accepted human weight. "I was in the gym, working out. I showered and changed as quickly as I could."

"No matter," Hennessey smiled.

"So, Charlotte . . . why the sudden interest, nearly twenty years on as well?"

"Well, sir, we are really looking at the safety of Melanie Clifford's conviction."

"I knew you were going to say that." Ffrench forced a smile. "It's probably prompted by the death of Cornelius Weekes – your interest, I mean."

"Yes," Hennessey replied. "Yes, it is."

"People who dig too deeply into the question of Melanie Clifford's conviction seem to have a habit of coming to a sticky end. They meet their maker before their time."

"People?" Hennessey's brow furrowed. "They?"

"People, they. Cornelius wasn't the first journalist to start asking awkward questions. There was another bloke, a chap called Donald Round. Now he was very quick off the mark, he was asking questions even before the appeal. Yes, Donald Round, and a much misnamed person he was. He was built like a slat, premature balding with thick-lensed spectacles. Not a great success with the ladies I would have thought, but I recall a sincerity that shone through and a brain that was all there. A young man who, like Cornelius, wanted to go somewhere in journalism and, like Cornelius, probably thought he had the story that could take him to Fleet Street.

"Donald was very badly beaten up in York one night and succumbed to his injuries forty-eight hours later without regaining consciousness. At the time I thought that it was a little suspect. Donald was hardly a thug – not the type to go out drinking and looking for a fight, and he was such a wimpish-looking bloke that he wouldn't have invited trouble on himself. I mean, there's no victory in knocking men like Donald Round to the deck – you don't score any points in thug culture for collecting the scalp of bookish blokes like Donald. Anyway, so I thought, and then I decided that there's no rules in York on Friday or Saturday night, and the most unlikely people get into punch-ups. Eventually I dismissed any connection between Donald's death and his interest in Melanie's conviction as being the stuff of fiction. But now that Cornelius has died in suspicious circumstances, and at about the same point that Donald was in his inquiries. They met Melanie's family, they met this family, they meet Melanie in prison, then they cross the line . . ."

"Where did they go after meeting Melanie?"

"That I can't tell you. But wherever it was that they went, they went to a dangerous place, by all accounts. Probably still is dangerous. I'd proceed with caution if I were you, gentlemen." Ffrench raised an eyebrow above a warm blue eye, a blue which matched his T-shirt, jeans and training shoes, all of which contrasted fiercely with the maroon embossed wallpaper and the darkly stained wood in the room; the tables, the cabinet, the double doors. "Being police officers, you might be safer, but 'safer' doesn't mean 'safe'."

"We'll bear that in mind, Mr Ffrench, thank you." Hennessey nodded. "Tell me, what specifically was the thrust of Cornelius Weekes' questions, and Donald Round's for that matter?"

"Well . . . both the same really. If I can recall Donald's

questions – he was here fourteen years ago. Yes, I think he wanted the same information as Cornelius. It was about Charlotte's relationship with Toby Erickson."

"And were you happy to talk about that?"

"Yes, though it was my parents who spoke to Donald. They've both gone downhill rapidly in the last ten years. They carried on, stoically so, after Charlotte's death, but the gap she left in our lives couldn't be filled and when the grave began to beckon them, neither seemed to resist it. Now they're counting the days until they are 'united with Charlotte', as father puts it. They were childhood sweethearts you know, married when they were twenty. I just know that when one goes, the other won't hang around. Charlotte's murder was the only real tragedy to befall either of them."

"But what a tragedy."

"As you say, Mr Hennessey, as you say."

"So, tell me, what was the quality of Charlotte's relationship with Toby Erickson?"

Benjamin Ffrench glanced up at the ornate plaster ceiling. "Where to begin . . . We didn't like it. You may as well know that we didn't approve of him – mother especially, she hated him. Even for a woman who had a lot of intuition, especially where the welfare of her only daughter was at issue, she just couldn't put her finger on why she didn't like him. The best she could come up with were words like 'creepy', 'skin crawling', 'oily' – words and phrases like that. By 'oily' I think she meant that you just couldn't get hold of his personality. I know what she meant – doubtless you'll meet him."

"By the sound of it, doubtless we will."

"If he hasn't changed, he'll appear as he ought to appear,

mannerisms and dress will be appropriate and as you'll probably expect them to be, but he seems to be acting rather than being. Trying to get hold of his personality will be like trying to nail jelly to a wall."

Hennessey smiled. He enjoyed the image.

"I . . . we . . . just couldn't get hold of him. I never saw him in an ill temper but I did get the impression of someone who could turn nasty in a trice. A bit like the false good humour of one or two publicans I can think of, or like that double-glazing salesman who tried to sell me double glazing for this house. Can you believe what a sale that would have been for him? Treated me like royalty, or as his best friend, until I said that 'I'd think about it', at which point he started to snarl and spit. I pointed out to him that his attitude had suddenly changed, to which he replied that he was only pleasant to people if they bought something from him."

"Blimey."

"That actually happened, and Toby Erickson put me in mind of that gentleman, who didn't make the sale."

"Yes, I think I know the type." Hennessey found himself warming to Benjamin Ffrench. "I'll make my own assessment of course, but that doesn't mean to say that I don't hear what you're saying."

"Of course."

"So, they weren't married very long?"

"No, you see Charlotte had recently returned from the tropics, came back not at all herself. Her personality appeared flatter than it had been when she left to go back-packing in India and South East Asia. She came back complaining of feeling tired all the time, couldn't muster any energy. Went to the medics of course and they did all sorts of tests but they couldn't find anything wrong."

"Which is of course not the same as saying there's nothing wrong."

"Exactly, it was some deep-rooted, insidious tropical illness that's there but won't show itself. But the point is that, as well as feeling tired, she tended to give in too easily. She became biddable due to her lack of energy . . . she became easily led . . . hadn't the energy to stand up for herself, or to resist pressure."

"I get the picture."

"So, Toby Erickson started calling, taking her out in his flash red sports car. He proposed indecently soon, we felt. She accepted."

"Because she was biddable?"

"We thought so . . . her heart was never in the marriage. So she married into the crumbling Erickson dynasty, taking a lot of money with her. As well as the money father settled on her when she married, she and I had also inherited a substantial sum from another relative. She paid her money into their joint account and six months later she was dead. But the Erickson dynasty stayed afloat and remained afloat."

"You're suspicious, Mr Ffrench?"

"Oh, I'm so pleased it shows. And now, in the eighteen years since her murder not one, but two, investigative reporters are murdered when trying to pry into the safety of Melanie Clifford's conviction. That's enough to make a saint suspicious, wouldn't you say? Especially since Erickson insisted that she was cremated."

"And you, Mr Ffrench, what are your thoughts on the matter? I ask because you don't sound convinced of the safety of Melanie Clifford's conviction yourself."

"Frankly I'm not and, as a family, we never were. But the pig-headed police officer in charge of the case was convinced and she was convicted, so we didn't press the matter, but father did speak to Melanie's relatives and said he was unhappy about the outcome of the trial. I think we felt it was up to Melanie's family to agitate about the issue. We just wanted to get on with our lives. But, as the years went on, we became more and more unhappy, the old doubts have resurfaced, which is why my parents were happy to help Donald and, in turn, I was happy to help Cornelius. We don't have anything we can go to the police with, and so helping reporters is all we can do. It's tragic that it seems to have led to two more murders. If the police don't get a result . . . well, I've already taken the decision not to help any subsequent journalist who may pick up on the story. It's not fair on them."

"Why do you doubt the safety of Melanie Clifford's conviction, just out of interest?" Hennessey was impressed by Benjamin Ffrench's ethics.

"Well, no one reason." Benjamin Ffrench relaxed back into his chair. "We knew Melanie and it just didn't, and still does not, ring true that she murdered Charlotte."

"You knew her?"

"Malton is a small place, only one or two families at this level of society, if you see what I mean. We are one, the Ericksons another – drink at the same golf club."

"I see."

"So we knew Toby Erickson before he and Charlotte became involved and, through him, we got to know Melanie, although I believe she lived in York."

"She did."

"Well, Melanie and Toby were involved with each other for about ten years."

"We understand it was an 'on' and 'off' sort of relationship."

"So it appeared. Frankly, I don't think Melanie was ever really serious about it. If they had got married it would have failed and I think she sensed that. When she did socialise with us in Malton, at the golf club, at the hunt balls, she always seemed to look awkward and gauche, out of her social depth. She would never have survived as Mrs Erickson in Malton. And Toby appeared in Charlotte's life when Melanie and Toby hadn't been seen in each other's company for a matter of months."

"So we understand."

"She's not a vindictive woman, she wasn't anyway. Though I shudder to think what twenty years in the slammer has done to her."

"But the journey from York to Malton on a dismal January night – there has to be a reason for that." Hennessey pressed Ffrench.

"Has there?" Ffrench shrugged. "Why has there? Why? You must be approaching retirement, Chief Inspector. I don't wish to be personal but you're clearly much nearer the end of your working life than the beginning."

"I am and I'm not at all unhappy about it." Hennessey smiled, but Ffrench saw the wounding and the wisdom intermingled in Hennessey's eyes.

"My point is that you look for motivation and reason and purpose. I should think that is the nature of a police officer's thinking. But I think you can look too far, too closely, too deeply, looking for something that isn't there. Sometimes there isn't a motivation. I recall Melanie as being similar to Charlotte, both were accommodating, easily put upon, biddable. I use the word again, but it's a very good one to describe both Charlotte and Melanie. Toby Erickson was, and remains, a pushy, overbearing individual, an insistent, persistent bully of a man, who needs biddable women. He wouldn't cope with a woman who could stand up to him. Put those two personalities together and I can see why Melanie would respond to an urgent sounding summons from Toby and would drive out to Malton despite the late hour and the weather. I can see that easily. Any other man wouldn't have summoned her; any other woman would have told him what to do with himself."

"But, as you say, put Toby and Melanie together – yes, you may be right, Mr Ffrench. Perhaps we are looking for something that really isn't there." Hennessey paused. "In fact, I'm beginning to see a lot of things that make me feel very uneasy." He glanced at his watch. Eleven a.m. A clock in the hall of the house chimed its confirmation of the time. He turned to Yellich. "Fancy a trip to Durham this afternoon?"

"Aye," Yellich nodded. "I think we better had, sir."

"You could only be going to visit Melanie?" Ffrench asked.

"It is our intention, yes."

"I don't know what's going to be said, but you could convey my kindest regards and also those of my parents."

Hennessey stood. "That's generous minded of you, sir."

"Not if you believe she's innocent." Ffrench also stood, as did Yellich.

At the front door of The Dower House, the police took their leave of Benjamin Ffrench with a warm shaking of hands.

Hennessey steeled himself and for the sake of expediency

ate, with a more eager Yellich, in the police canteen, despite the promise he had made to himself the previous day. Something which purported to be meat pie and chips, and something which purported to be plum pudding and custard passed for his lunch and was obliged to sustain him until dinner. After their meal, Hennessey and Yellich both agreed that the most civilised way to travel between York and Durham was by rail, especially given the close proximity of the railway stations in either city to Micklegate Bar Police Station on the one hand, and Durham gaol on the other.

At York railway station, a vast glass canopy over curved platforms, they took tea at the 'Lemon Tree' on platform nine, while waiting for the royal blue liveried GNER's, "slightly delayed arrival calling at Darlington, Durham, Newcastle, Berwick upon Tweed and Edinburgh."

Hennessey and Yellich sat side by side during the journey, passing it in silence, each content to enjoy the view of flat, lush countryside and the speedy, smooth ride.

Hennessey had never before been to Durham Station and found himself impressed and interested by it, perched, it seemed, atop a hill overlooking the small city, at the northern end of a viaduct. He saw it only comprised an up platform and a down platform with a single relief line between the two main lines. He saw it clearly as a bottleneck on the main east coast, London to Edinburgh line, and he was not surprised to see the platform staff hurry their train's departure upon the completed egress and ingress of passengers.

Hennessey and Yellich walked down the curving road to the traffic roundabout and crossed into Millburngate Shopping Centre and entered the steep, pedestrianised Silver Street. At once Hennessey noted great similarities between York and Durham, both really just small towns but enjoying city status; both with impressive cathedrals, both seats of law and learning, both attracting tourists. Turning sharp right at Market Square, they crossed the River Wear by Elvet Bridge and found themselves in the spill of the prison.

HM Prison vehicles could be seen in greater frequency driving along Old Elvet between the solid nineteenth-century buildings, groups of men and women in white shirts and black ties – clearly prison staff and, thought Hennessey, clearly needing each other – were walking in either direction along the pavement. In the garden in front of the Law Courts, family groups or individuals stood, or sat in the shade of the shrubs, each with a hard, embittered look about him or her, yea, even unto the children. And many eyed Hennessey and Yellich with open hostility: prisoners' families awaiting the commencement of afternoon visiting hours had recognised the stamp of 'police' about the two men.

Hennessey and Yellich walked smartly side by side, passed the Crown Court Building, following the road as it climbed to the right as Old Elvet became Whinneyhill, though it was nonetheless the same continuous stretch of tarmac. To their left the ground fell away beyond the angular construction that was the Magistrates' Court, down to the well-tended racecourse/university playing fields. Beyond the sports fields was the river and beyond that the landscape rose steeply as a thickly foliaged embankment from which buildings protruded.

Yellich glanced at the prison which came into view as he and Hennessey turned the corner. He gazed at the pale grey stone edifice under a roof of darker grey slate and the blue steel doors of the entrance. Yellich then glanced to his left and pondered the irony of the sporting facilities belonging to one of Britain's most prestigious universities, abutting one of Britain's most feared gaols – separated only by a narrow road.

In the prison, after their identities had been checked and the formalities of signing in were over, Hennessey and Yellich were escorted through the main visiting area, at that moment vacant. It was a large room of low tables in neat rows, fixed to the floor. Around each table were four chairs, also fixed to the floor. Against the wall was a hot drinks vending machine.

The prison officer, a tall, silver-haired man of jovial personality who spoke in a warm Geordie accent, escorted Hennessey and Yellich down a narrow corridor beyond the visiting area, through a series of lockable metal grill doors and out into the yard, beyond which was clearly the nineteenth-century part of the gaol. They walked down the sloping yard to a door set in a twenty-foot high wire fence topped with curling razor wire. At the gate the prison officer spoke into a microphone and identified himself, at which point the gate was opened by remote control. The prison officer pushed the gate open and, all three walked through the gateway. The prison officer closed it and it locked automatically. They turned right, through another gate set in another high fence and entered the female prisoners' unit where Hennessey and Yellich were asked to wait in one of the agents' rooms. There they they sat side by side again, but this time in a room bare, save for a table and four chairs under a window of thick opaque glass.

"I feel fear," Hennessey broke the silence.

"Fear? Not like you, skipper."

"It's curious, I didn't think I would feel this. Whatever I thought I'd feel, fear was the last thing I anticipated."

"Because she may have been innocent all along?"

Hennessey nodded. "Yes. That's exactly what I do mean."

Then came the sound of doors opening and clanging shut from outside the room, the tapping of a stick on a corridor floor. The door of the agents' room opened and a blonde – and to Yellich's more youthful eye – and not at all unattractive female prison officer guided Melanie Clifford to one of the vacant chairs opposite Hennessey and Yellich.

Both man felt the other's dismay. So this, each thought, was Melanie Clifford whom His Lordship had thought so ill of that he had sentenced her to a minimum of twenty years imprisonment before she could be considered for parole. This monster in the eyes of the press was in real life short, frail and finely made, wearing well for her fifty-five years. Though prison life can be a physically healthy one – little tobacco, no alcohol – psychologically speaking, Hennessey knew that it was strictly a one-way ticket, especially after a ten stretch or longer. And Melanie Clifford had been inside longer than that, much longer, nearly twice as much longer.

She was blind. She stared straight ahead and like all people who lose their sight, she was very image conscious, looking as smart as prison wear would allow: loose blouse, jeans and soft-soled shoes, her hair neat and her face and hands scrubbed clean. It was Hennessey's observation that people who are born blind have no sense of image, seeing their image either in a mirror or in a photograph has not been their experience. People who are born blind have no sense of style, or colour, but dress for comfort and practicality and tend to walk holding their head on one side to maximise the efficiency of their hearing. Melanie Clifford, having been born sighted, kept herself smart, and stared straight ahead, and folded her white stick and slid it out of sight up her shirt sleeve.

Oddly, Hennessey found a small part of himself hoping that she was guilty all along, because if so, she would only have a harsh sentence to complain about, but if she was innocent . . . the implications . . . nothing, nothing, no amount of money could compensate. "Melanie," he spoke softly.

"Miss Clifford, if you don't mind." And the blind, frail, finely made body instantly showed that it contained a personality which, if once 'biddable', was now made of steel. Hennessey smiled and thought 'good for you'.

"Miss Clifford, I am Detective Chief Inspector Hennessey and with me is Detective Sergeant Yellich, both of the North Yorkshire Police, based at Micklegate Bar Police Station in York."

"Yes, I know where Micklegate Bar Police Station is. I'm glad you said 'with me', so often people have said 'this is' but 'this is' is something that you can only say to a sighted person. So thank you for your sensitivity."

"Yes . . ." Hennessey felt awkward.

"You're here because of Cornelius Weekes?"

"Yes, we are."

"I phoned my sister this morning. I earn money with which to buy phone cards. She told me about your visit and I heard about Cornelius on the news, and in the newspapers. One of the women in here reads the paper to me. Did you know that Cornelius was the second newspaperman to take an interest in my case, and that the first one was also murdered?"

"Yes, we know that."

"I had sight when the first visited me. Donald Round, a nice lad, but no street fighter. When I heard that he'd had the life kicked out of him one night in an alley in central York, I knew, I just knew that it wasn't an incident of random violence. Then police said he was in the wrong place at the wrong time and that such things happen, and that they weren't looking any further. At first I accepted it, shock, I suppose, but within a few hours I thought there was more to it. You know, in here you get to do an awful lot of thinking and I soon realised that Donald wasn't in the wrong place at the wrong time – he was in fact in the right place at the right time. Exactly where and when someone wanted him to be."

"Set up, you think?"

"Set up, I know. I mean in myself I know, in my waters I know. But who by? Well, that I don't know. What do you know about Donald's murder?"

"No more than you do, we only found out about it this morning. Benjamin Ffrench told us about him. He too clearly has his suspicions."

"Benjamin . . . yes."

"He asked us to convey his regards."

"That's good of him."

"If it's any comfort, he believes that you are innocent."

"And what do you believe, Inspector?"

"I . . . we . . . are keeping an open mind, but having said that, we are beginning to see reasons to have a second look at the murder of Charlotte Erickson."

"I only want my conviction quashed. If my conviction is quashed, I can be buried on sanctified ground. That's all I want. A burial in a churchyard. That's all I want. Money on the scale of a lottery win won't, can't, compensate for the lost years, and my blindness has no pathological base, nothing for the medics to address – if I am shown to be innocent . . ."

"Are you?" Hennessey snapped.

"Yes!" Melanie Clifford's reply was equally rapid. "If I am shown to be innocent, which I am, that doesn't mean to say that my sight will miraculously return."

"Yes, I'm very sorry about your sight. I only wish—"

"Well, wishing won't help," Melanie Clifford sighed. "But you know, I feel guilty . . . I didn't murder Charlotte, I don't feel guilty about that but I feel responsible for the deaths of Donald and Cornelius. I have something to complain about, the loss of liberty and the loss of sight, but two young men may, no probably have, lost their lives trying to fight my corner. They may have wanted something for themselves, a story that would form the basis of a career in journalism, but I believe the motive for both men was to expose a miscarriage of justice. And, you know, the fact that someone is prepared to kill to prevent a secret being exposed – doesn't that tell you something?"

"It does. I'm not sure what, though."

"You haven't read any files or reports about Donald's death?"

"Not yet."

"Well, I'll tell you what I know, what I remember. He lived in Malton, worked for the local newspaper . . . he was a small, thin man, bespectacled, yet he goes into York one night and is found beaten to death up a snickelway. Ought to make the police sit up, wouldn't you think? But instead, they came up with the 'wrong place at the wrong time' number."

"Well, we can't comment, not having read the file."

"Fair enough, but I believe he was keeping a rendezvous. Set up, as you say. I believe he was lured to York to be silenced. In his eagerness for a good story, he threw caution to the wind, and it cost him his life."

"Do you have any idea who'd do it? Or any of the murders?"

"I don't, not even who killed Charlotte, because Toby was away that night – the house was empty, no lights, nothing, but Toby definitely called me. I'm sure it was Toby, I wouldn't mistake his voice, but when I got to the house, there was nobody there."

"All right, let's talk about that night, as you remember it, the events as you recall them."

Melanie Clifford smiled. "If you like, but I won't deviate from my statement, but first shall I tell you what it's like in here?"

"If you like – but for what reason?"

"For this reason. Because we are unlocked at eight a.m., then locked up again from twelve 'til one so the staff can have lunch, then we're locked up again from five till six so the staff can have an evening meal, then we're locked up for the night at eight p.m. There's an education block which teaches basic skills, like reading and writing, and also computer skills, which is of little use to me because I am – what is the phrase? – 'visually challenged'. There is an exercise yard which is small, small, small. If you can imagine three buses being arranged so that they form a triangle then that is the shape and size of the exercise yard, with walls thirty feet high on two sides and on the third side is a wire fence, and just beyond that is another wire fence and beyond that is a wall. Yet we value our little exercise yard, even I do, because it's the only source of natural light in the female wing. All windows are opaque or frosted, all other light is artificial. Our hair darkens in here, no sunlight you see, yet in our little exercise yard, we can look up and see the sky. They can look up and see the sky. When I could see, I used to live for the hour in the exercise yard each day, now it's total darkness with no activity except Braille books. All I do is lie on my bed in my cell and re-live the events of 'that night', as you call it. And also about my trial, which I think I can remember word for word."

"Your brother-in-law said the same."

"He and my sister were very supportive. Still are. Anyway I was happy, utterly unperturbed about going to trial. I had faith in the British criminal justice system. At the trial the prosecution painted such a picture of me that even my worst enemy would be hard put to recognise me: apparently I was a vindictive, cold-blooded, premeditated murderer. Shooting a woman still in the bud of life because she had got what I couldn't have. Throughout the trial, the judge kept glaring at me – it must have swayed the jury – and my barrister, not a man with fire in his belly, tended to fight by smiling at the judge instead of arguing my case. He hardly put up a fight at all. When the jury said 'guilty', I just went into shock and didn't seem to hear the sentence at the time. I can hear it now, though, word for word. The appeal court upheld the conviction and it was soon after that that I went blind in my sleep, but I was still such a security risk that I had to be taken to hospital handcuffed to a warder with two other warders in attendance. To be fair, I sensed the warders were a bit embarrassed but Home Office regulations have to be observed."

"So," Hennessey relaxed back in his chair, "I'm sorry about the way you have to live."

"Exist."

"And I repeat, I'm sorry for your blindness. But don't let your anger get in the way of helping yourself. Neither I nor Sergeant Yellich had any part in your prosecution, and we've come a long way to see you. Help yourself by giving us something which will cause us to look again at Charlotte's murder."

"All right . . . sorry . . . I shouldn't be angry at you. Right, it was quite late, well late to ask a sudden drop-everything-and-do-it-now sort of favour. It was about nine or ten. I'd settled down for the evening, the dog had been exercised and then the phone rang. It was Toby. He said he was in trouble and that he needed help urgently. Could I come to the farm?"

"He said 'come'?"

"Yes. That's why I assumed he was at the farm, so I was knocked sideways when I heard his alibi, that he was in Edinburgh at the time, on business. Anyway, I went – it's not a farm any more you understand, he sold off all the farmland save for about five acres which he turned into gardens round the farmhouse, but it's still called Coles Copse Farm. Coles Copse is on the original farmland, a stand of trees of about a quarter of an acre."

"I see."

"So I drove there, it may seem odd but I did."

"It does seem a little strange," Hennessey conceded. "It always did seem a strange thing to do."

"The scorned woman who goes to her ex-fiancé's house at his behest, the scorned woman who is still prepared to do her betrayer's least bidding. Is that what you mean, Chief

Inspector? The prosecution lawyer, *he* really had a fire in his belly and he made so much of that. 'Beyond belief' he called my explanation, he also said it 'beggars belief'. He really rammed the point home. 'Strains credibility' was yet another phrase he employed, oh yes, 'strains credibility up to and beyond breaking point', that was it. Lawyers have a way with words."

"They have, that's true, and yes, Miss Clifford, that's what I do mean."

Melanie Clifford leaned forward. "Well, in the first place, I wasn't a scorned woman, as my brother-in-law has probably told you."

"He did, in fact, but we'd like to hear it from you."

"Well, all right, hear it from me. Toby and I would never have got married, not ever. We had woven in and out of each other's lives for about ten years, but it was never really serious, it was more a mutual convenience – two lonely people accepting each other because there was no one else, or until someone else came along. And that was just the way of it. We had drifted apart before Charlotte came on the scene, so he didn't reject me for her, despite what m'learned friend for the Crown had the ladies and gentlemen of the jury believe. It wasn't like that, which my beaming beach bum of a barrister could have told them if he had had a mind to do so. So that's the first point. The second point is that Toby and I retained a friendship, so much so, that when he and Charlotte announced their engagement, I sent a card to congratulate them."

"So we understand."

"I visited them once or twice after they married, and settled down to the not unpleasant, uncomplicated life of a spinster with the intention of allowing myself to drift apart from Toby and Charlotte. The single life has its advantages. I loved my little house, my dog and cat, pottering about – so peaceful, especially when I heard or read about all those bloody divorces."

"I can sympathise with that," Hennessey smiled, knowing that a smile can be 'heard'.

"Can you? Are you a single man?"

"In a sense. Strictly speaking I'm a very long-term widower."

"I'm sorry . . . but you can understand then, I wasn't envious of Charlotte."

"Yes, I can understand, but please carry on."

"I'm not the same person I was then. I've hardened up. Had to, couldn't have survived otherwise. Back then I realise that I used to let myself be put upon. Wouldn't stand up for myself, and Toby has a pushy nature, very demanding. Then it was as if I was a robot, all Toby had to do was just push a button and I'd respond. That night, when the phone rang, I'd just settled down for the evening in front of a live fire – I used to burn wood in the hearth. I loved real fire, controlled of course; a fire is a good friend. The phone rang and I knew, I just knew that it was going to be Toby and I knew he was going to ask me a favour and I knew I was going to say 'yes'. I knew I was going to agree to do whatever he was going to ask me to do."

"Which is what happened?"

"Which is what happened, as you say. He asked me to come to the farm because 'there's a problem'. He didn't say what it was but he was very insistent. So I agreed, a half-hour drive on a cold, wet January night – you know what winters are like in the Vale. You know, the wind had died down the following morning, when I was arrested, the air was very still. Do you know, that night was the last time I felt wind in my face or tugging at my hair. That's something else you don't get in maximum security – no climate change to speak of. I suppose that goes hand in hand with next to no natural light. Sometimes it's sunny in the exercise yard, sometimes there's a bit of drizzle, but never any wind, the wind blows over the top, so for the most part it's central heating and electric lighting."

"So you got to the Erickson house. Then what?"

"It was in darkness. I thought that was a little odd, strange in fact. It wasn't really very late, only about ten p.m.. Rang the doorbell, no reply, rang it a few times then. I got a bit curious, walked to the side of the house, round the back, round the other side of the house and back to where I'd parked my car: all round the house, no lights, no noise, just a big old house in a stormy night, wind swaying the trees and wires howling in the wind."

"Wires?"

"Electric cables which ran from the house to the out-buildings."

"I see. No other movement or sound?"

"No, just the trees swaying and the wires howling. Didn't know what to do, so I went home. Don't tell me that I should have phoned the police. I know that now. I can't tell you how many times I have lain on my bed saying 'should have phoned the police, should have phoned the police'. The combination of the phone call and a dark, empty house which should have had lights on and people inside was suspicious enough for me to have gone to the police, but I didn't. I just didn't. It would have been all right for me then, but I didn't and it's cost me eighteen years of my life, plus my sight. Anyway, I drove home, went to bed – I was feeling sleepy by then. The next morning I was woken by a hammering on the door. It was the boys in blue, demanding the keys to my car and shouting at me to get dressed. After that it was all a bit of a whirl."

"Tell me about the police questioning."

"It was more like an interrogation. I know things are different now – taped interviews, solicitors present but then it was two cops trying to make me confess to something I didn't do. One, a large, well-built man, was called Cross and cross was his temperament. Didn't actually hit me but I think he came close to it. If I'd been a twentysomething man . . . I think . . . well he didn't actually resort to physical violence but, like I said, he came close. Very close. He wouldn't listen to me, kept going on and on 'you did it, you did it . . . didn't you . . . you're lying to us . . . we know you did it', like that, he never let up. I felt like actually admitting to it, just to stop the battering, but I didn't. They said they'd spoken to Toby and he denied making any call to me at all. I understand from new arrivals in here that you can now dial 1471 to get the number that called you last."

"You can, if it hasn't been shielded. You can do that if the call is made from a private or commercial phone, but not from a pay phone."

"I see – well anyway, that wasn't available then. Toby's phone call was the last phone call I received. Toby also had an alibi; he was at a business conference in Edinburgh. It was when I heard that, that I realised I'd been set up."

"By who?"

"Toby, who else? It's remarkable that I still call him by his first name. It suggests approval – I should be calling him 'Erickson', or 'that man' – but that's just part of me, I suppose, the same part of me that drives out to deserted houses late at night in January at someone else's request. Anyway, they found the murder weapon in my car, wiped clean of fingerprints, so that meant I had something to hide, so said big Mr Cross.

"They kept me in the police cells that night, gave me food of sorts – what was supposed to have been a hot meal but it had practically grown cobwebs by the time they let me have it. It was just another ploy to wear me down. It felt like fighting an army of driver ants, one insect wouldn't be a problem, but thousands of them, millions . . . Or bees. One isn't a problem, but thousands of them and they're all killer bees. One police ploy isn't a problem, but half a dozen. Then your mind starts to play tricks and you wonder if you really did shoot someone.

"The following day they showed me photographs of Charlotte's body and next to it was a man's footprint, so I said, 'Look, that's not my footprint, I don't have any shoes like that, that's industrial footwear and too big for my feet – surely you want the person who left that footprint?'"

"Wait a minute." Hennessey glanced at Yellich, who grimaced. "Are you telling us that you pointed out that footprint to John Cross?"

"John? So that's his Christian name is it? But yes, I pointed out the footprint to Mr Cross the cross policeman."

"And he said?"

"He said it wasn't relevant, told me it was there before the body was dumped. I mean to say, however, he could have known that I wouldn't have known, but that's what he said. 'It doesn't matter about the footprint, just look at what you've done.' That's what he said."

"Was there just you and John Cross in the room at that moment?"

"No . . . no, there was another officer, quite young."

"You don't recall his name? It doesn't matter if you can't, it'll be in the file."

"No, I don't but he wasn't a Yorkshireman, he was Welsh judging by his accent, though I believe the Western Isles accent sounds more Welsh than Scottish, but I think he was Welsh. He had a tuft of blonde hair growing amid the black hair on his scalp."

Hennessey and Yellich turned to each other and said together, "Daffyd Jones."

"You know him?"

"Yes. He is a Welshman. And he's still around, in a manner of speaking. Did you mention the footprints to your solicitor?"

"Yes, and also to the barrister. But he didn't mention it in the trial." Melanie Clifford paused. "But I wasn't frightened. Not once – even during the trial I felt safe. I was sure I was going to be acquitted. Now I just feel betrayed by the whole rotten lousy self-serving system. Especially after the appeal failed."

"Miss Clifford," Hennessey spoke softly, "you have had a lot of time to think about what happened – a great deal of time."

"You can say that again, eighteen years, almost to the day. Yes, I was arrested in January, tried in May of that year, sentence backdated to the day of my arrest. So you know how long that is in days? I'll tell you. It's six thousand five hundred and seventy, that's nineteen thousand seven hundred and ten meals, assuming three meals a day. Since losing my sight I keep my brain agile by doing mental arithmetic. So yes, you could say that I've had a great deal of time to think about it."

"So, within these four walls, what do you think happened?"

"So, within these four walls . . . Toby married Charlotte only for her money because his business was sinking. When her money was safely in their joint account and she was of no further use to him, he murdered her. It's calculating and extreme, but that's Toby Erickson, and image is important to him, and Charlotte couldn't cut it in that respect. I dare say she would have considered herself attractive but she was mentally ill. Did you know that?"

"Her brother said she had contracted some rare tropical illness which the medics couldn't treat and which would lay her low from time to time."

Melanie Clifford smiled. "That's the proud Ffrench family being unprepared to admit to the stigma of mental ill-health in the family. The policy of locking the barking mad daughter in the attic, or the cellar . . . insanity might exist, but not in one of theirs, don't you know. It's true that Charlotte did travel to exotic places, but it is my understanding that she had a breakdown on her return. It may have been triggered by the travelling, it may have been about to happen all along, but the upshot is that it left her a dull, flat, personality, without any 'effect' as I believe it's called. It was as though she'd had a lobotomy."

"I see."

"You'd ask her a question and she'd encapsulate the question in her reply, such as . . . you'd say, 'Hello, Charlotte, it's a nice day today' and she would reply in a monotone and with a dull, glazed look in her eyes: 'Hello, yes, it's a nice day today.' I think that, despite what they might have said, the Ffrenches were really quite delighted when Toby Erickson offered to take their embarrassment off their hands, and a handsome dowry was the manifestation of said delight and gratitude. But Toby's problem was that he wanted the money Charlotte brought with her but not Charlotte. She just was not a businessman's wife. If you ask me a divorce was out of the question, financially speaking, so the answer was a bullet in the head. How he did it and managed to be in Edinburgh at the same time I don't know, can't answer that one, nor can I tell you how the rifle came to be in the boot of my car which I always kept locked. Can't answer that one either."

Hennessey remained silent.

"But somebody had to carry the can. Erickson had succeeded in luring me to the crime scene, and by some means he had the rifle put in my car, and all the police wanted was a motive and Toby – I mean Erickson – provided them with that, the old scorned woman number. It all appealed to John Cross and he locked on to me like a heat-seeking missile. The issue of the footprint meant nothing to him, the fact that I wasn't a scorned woman meant nothing. I don't know how to shoot a rifle, that didn't mean anything to him. So here's me in my small, dark world, and another two years to go before I get considered for parole. And even then it's only a consideration. I could be in here for another ten years yet."

"And the two journalists? Donald Round and Cornelius Weekes. What do you think happened there?"

"Well they wouldn't be the first two reporters to get too near the truth for their own safety. I imagine they got too near to some item of evidence that linked Erickson to Charlotte's murder and so he bumped them off. Poor Donald's death was made to look like random violence, a mindless attack one night, and Cornelius, well I heard that an attempt was made to dress that up to look like a suicide."

"That's right."

"Didn't fool the boys in blue, though, did it? Pity the boys in blue couldn't have been a bit more astute eighteen years ago."

Later, standing side by side on the up platform of Durham Station, amid a group of fellow passengers, it was Yellich who, staring straight ahead, broke the silence between them. "It's a solemn business, skipper, solemn, solemn, solemn, and no mistake."

Hennessey drove home to his house in Easingwold. He felt depressed, awkward, gauche, and a heavy sensation seemed to weigh on his stomach as though he'd overindulged in too much food. As he approached his house on Thirsk Road, he smiled as he recognised a silver BMW parked on the kerb outside his house. "Charles," he said to himself.

He turned into the driveway and saw a young man standing on the back lawn throwing a ball for Oscar to retrieve, then both dog and man turned at the sound of Hennessey's car, and walked happily to the fence which ran from the house to the garage. Hennessey left his car and walked towards them. The men shook hands as Hennessey fondled Oscar's ears.

"This is new." The younger man patted the fence.

"Put it up on a whim. It allows my best friend here to have the run of the garden while I'm out. Had a dog-flap fitted too. Better than leaving him cooped up inside the house. I'll let myself in and join you."

"I'll put the spare key back under the rock before I forget." Charles Hennessey entered the house by the rear door, passed his father in the hall, exited the house by the front door and placed the spare key, wrapped in a plastic bag, under a rock in the shadow of the privet in the front garden. He returned to the house and joined George Hennessey in the kitchen as the latter filled the kettle.

"Getting there, I see." Charles Hennessey held up a sheet of paper of paper containing surnames in alphabetical order, with a generous space between each name.

"Yes, up to twenty-seven now. Getting there, the same thirty-two names were shouted out each morning for five years and I can remember all but five. That's a trifle annoying but I'll get there. I remembered the bulk of the names on the day I decided to do the exercise, the others came to mind in ones or twos over the next few weeks."

"But five elude you. The infamous five."

"Five elude me." Hennessey put a teapot, two mugs and a jug of milk on a tray. "Come on, let's sit outside, can't waste a beautiful evening like this by sitting indoors."

Outside on the patio, the two men sat sipping tea as the sun sank over a wide landscape, and Oscar explored the shaded areas of the garden. They enjoyed each other's company, father and son. They didn't need to talk, but the silence was eventually broken by Hennessey senior. "What are you doing at the moment?"

"I'm leading at Teeside. Were going N.G. to a case of serious assault plus possession for intention to supply: 'I definitely did not pick up the hammer and fracture the man's skull despite what three impartial witnesses of good character might say. And the class A drug subsequently found both in my car and my place of residence was for my use only' – despite the quantity of said class A drug, which was sufficient to keep the drug culture in the Middlesborough area going for six months." Charles Hennessey sipped his tea. "He just won't see sense and so often that's the case. With that weight of evidence, the best thing do is to admit it, collect five years, out in three, but going N.G. he's looking at ten years. You nail 'em, I get them off . . . but not this time, this time the police will get a 'result', as I believe is the expression."

"It is, and a good result is a police officer's delight. So, children well?"

"Thriving, annoyingly so, but I wouldn't have missed the experience for the world . . . the miracle of birth. I have a partner, though, and I often think that it must have been hard for you to bring me up alone."

"It was, but I had help from time to time and I wouldn't have missed the experience for the world either."

"Yes . . . how is the present relationship?"

"Well . . . yes, it's well. We've settled down very well now, no chance of us merging households though. We've talked it over and have decided that at our age, it wouldn't be a sensible move. Things are best left as they are, leave well alone. If it ain't broke, don't fix it."

After a further prolonged silence Charles Hennessey said. "Dad, is something bothering you? You seem distant, preoccupied somehow."

"Yes, I am." Hennessey put his mug on the tray. "I am, I confess. In fact I am deeply worried that we may have uncovered a dreadful miscarriage of justice. If we have, it's nothing that the police or the Bar are going to be proud of, if it does turn out that the wrong person was convicted."

"Well, that does happen from time to time and we are

terrified of it. There's nothing frightens a criminal lawyer more than an unsafe conviction."

"This person has been banged up for the last eighteen years." George Hennessey said softly as a swallow swooped over the lawn.

"Oh. What did he do, steal the Crown Jewels?"

"*She*, she allegedly murdered someone."

"And she's still inside – had to be premeditated."

"Oh it was, very premeditated, but I don't think she did it. Perfunctory performance by her defence counsel, victim was a recently married woman, held up to be a rival in love, and a hanging judge – and none of this was helped by her not guilty plea which was made despite what appeared to be, but only appeared to be, strong evidence to the contrary. All added up to life with the recommendation that she should serve a minimum of twenty summers and winters as a guest of Her Majesty. I met her this afternoon, she'd worked out the number of meals she would eat in the twenty-year period. I can't recall the number, but it was well – quite a lot."

"As it would be."

"But the thing that is beginning to hang over me like a black cloud is that evidence of her innocence was actually captured in the scene-of-crime photographs. At the very least it points to an accomplice, something which the Crown failed to address and, at the most, it points to the crime being committed by a male."

"Oh no."

"Oh yes. And it, a footprint in the soil beside the corpse, was pointed out to the investigating police officer who dismissed it and to the defence counsel who didn't mention it."

"Oh."

"Is the minimum that could be said in such circumstances. At the beginning of this week I held the officer in question in high regard. Now I have to accept that he just refused to 'see' evidence, that he closed his mind to it because he was convinced of the woman's guilt, or that he wilfully perverted the course of justice. One or the other."

"Oh dear, oh dear, oh dear."

"Solemn, as my sergeant said. Very, very solemn."

Five

In which Hennessey preys upon the conscience of a Welshman, hears of two burnt-out cases and Yellich passes a pleasant and profitable afternoon in Malton.

THURSDAY

"It might not come to it, Commander." Hennessey spoke softly as he watched the colour drain from Sharkey's face.

"It sounds like it already has, George. We mustn't fool ourselves, this is no time for ostrich-like behaviour." Sharkey sat still in his chair, almost impassively, thought Hennessey. In fact the only display of emotion was the colour draining from the man's face. And the look in his eyes. A look of disbelief leading to despair.

Sharkey was a short man for a police officer – clearly, Hennessey assumed, to have been deemed so full of the 'right stuff' that a lack of an inch or two was thought to be a price worth paying. A photograph on the wall behind him spoke of time spent as an officer in the British Army, a second photograph showed him as an officer in the Royal Hong Kong Police.

"I fully agree with that attitude, sir, but I also have to make sure of my ground."

"Of course, but it sounds bad. Sounds very bad indeed. He'll be retired now, maybe even deceased. I never knew him, did you?"

"Only by reputation, sir. The reputation of a man who he got results."

"He certainly got those all right, the question now being is, by what methods did he get his results? And how valid were they?"

"We'll have to look at his other cases."

"No, we won't."

Hennessey felt his jaw slacken. Commander Sharkey, the stickler for all things right, Sharkey, the man who made no secret of his near pathological terror of corruption in the force, was here, advocating a cover-up? Surely, Hennessey thought, surely not. But he said nothing.

"What I mean is, George, is that if Cross did betray the integrity of the police force, then there'll be more adverse publicity than we dare fear, even in our worst nightmares. When that happens, all the punters who feel they were knifed by Cross will come banging on our door, or their solicitors will do that for them. Then we'll have to look at each case that demands that it be re-looked at. It's probably unfair to do it like that, but it's pragmatic. We don't have the manpower to do what you suggest, much as I would like to and much as that may disappoint you. We simply can't take the initiative. We'll respond to complaints about Cross, but we can't launch an investigation into his career."

A pause.

"You're disappointed George, probably more than you're showing?"

"Yes, sir, I am, but I don't know what about. But I won't argue with your policy on this matter, not least because it makes sense given our limited resources."

"Thank you." Sharkey smiled briefly. "So what's your next step?"

"Well, John Cross had an oppo at the time, a Welsh bloke, Daffyd Jones. He's left the force now and he might be prepared to speak more freely about Cross because of it. I'll visit him, I think."

"If there is anything to speak about . . . but in my waters, George. You know, after my time in Hong Kong, I saw enough police corruption to last me out. I know I am obsessed by it and how tiresome that can be for my senior officers, but I was on the look-out for bribes and payoffs. I never thought there'd be an issue of perverting the course of justice. Just goes to show."

"As you say, sir, you never can tell." Hennessey made to stand.

"Wait a minute." Sharkey held up his hand and Hennessey settled back in his chair. "George, I've been wanting to have a chat to you for a while – no aspersion is being cast, none whatsoever."

"But . . . ?" Hennessey felt worried.

"George, as well as corruption, I have another fear that keeps me awake at night. It stems from my school days and you are not the first man in this Division that I've said this to, so as well as no aspersion, there is also no singling out."

"I'm relieved to hear it."

"When I was in my final year at school our very able maths teacher left to take up another post at another school – bettering himself, I should think. That meant there was no one to take final-year maths. There was another teacher at the school, he was respected by the pupils. William Taighe was his name and he was so respected that he didn't get any of the unkind nicknames that some of the other staff got. We just called him 'Billy Taighe'. He was in his sixties."

"Tay? As in 'silvery Tay'?"

"T-a-i-g-h-e. Looking back he really should have been a primary school teacher and he usually taught the less able or younger forms. Anyway he was given, and I suspect coerced or bullied into taking, final-year maths. You know, George, he couldn't understand the work. He'd collapse in the middle of a lesson. I don't mean he'd fall over, I mean he'd get halfway through a problem and then couldn't take it any further – didn't know what the next step was. I once remember him doing that and he went to sit on the desk of a very able boy and said 'Where do you think we should go from here, Robert?'. Can you imagine the man's humiliation? Asking Billy Taighe to take on that work was . . . well, it was like taking the payload from the back of an articulated lorry and putting it on the back of a milk float, it was like asking a ten-year-old to carry an infantryman's rifle and pack."

"I get the picture, sir."

"One of the other things he was doing at the time was preparing another form for a certificate which was based on exam plus course-work called a 'project'. No project, no certificate, no matter how well you did in the exam. Anyway, the day that the projects had to be handed in came and not one boy in that form had done his project and there was no time to cobble something together at the last minute. So there he was, unable to understand maths at the level he was required to teach it, and all but one of the other form weren't going to get their certificate."

"Poor man."

"You do feel for him, don't you? But you see, he was burnt out. All he was saying to the other form was 'everybody's doing their project. . . good. . . any problems, let me know. He genuinely believed he was doing his job, because he hadn't the energy left to ensure that that form did their project work in class. That's a symptom of burn-out, believing in your heart of hearts that you're doing the job but in fact you're falling well short."

"Commander, I hope—"

"Let me finish, George. There's nothing for you to worry about. But you see what really annoys me about this story was that Billy Taighe was overweight, had a red face, a red nose, and smoked like a chimney. He'd even walk into the corridor and stay out of the class for a few minutes and come back nipping a fag. But think about it — overweight, middle-aged, blood pressure up, red nose. He was probably drinking each evening, smoking heavily, a job he couldn't do . . . all those signals he was giving out and none of his colleagues picked up that he was struggling. Nobody picked up that he was a heart attack waiting to happen. But that's what happened, when he found that virtually nobody in the other form had done his project, he blew up at them, went home and keeled over with a massive coronary."

"Not a good end to a life."

"I find myself thinking about him and his story often and, frankly, I wouldn't have my old headmaster's conscience for a lottery win. I firmly believe, George, that people should coast to a deserved retirement, they shouldn't be worked when exhausted, they should be allowed to soft-pedal until their last working day."

"Sir—"

127

"George, you do not strike me as struggling, your appearance is that of a healthy man, your performance is not only up to scratch, it is a model for more junior officers. But what happened to Billy Taighe won't happen to any of my staff. Your retirement is on the horizon, if you want out of the field, you only have to say the word."

Hennessey stood. "Since you put it like that, sir, I'm not offended, but thanks, but no thanks. I'll keep in the field until I retire."

"It was a bit of a gamble, at the time I had cause to question my sanity, but it's paid off, so far anyway." Daffyd Jones, silk shirt and expensive-looking suit, sat on a leather-bound chair in front of a neat 'everything in its place' desk. He had medieval offices: cramped, low ceiling, small windows – which offered a glimpse of the Minster glowing in the sun – wood panelling, sober-coloured, deep-pile carpet. "Mind you, the pension, the job security . . . there are times when I can't sleep at night, my mind tends to turn on what I gave up."

"But you seem to be doing all right though, Daffyd." Hennessey glanced round the office, smiling approvingly. Yellich did the same.

"Well, business is good at the moment," Jones placed a meaty hand on his desk top beside his computer, "touch wood. Business is good, very good. I've got a staff of twenty-one people. I'm taking on two more at the beginning of next month."

"Never thought of returning to the Valleys, Daffyd?"

"Bit difficult for me to return to the Valleys. I'm from North Wales, boyo, but the answer's 'no'. I married a Yorkshire lass, got children settled in school in York, contacts are all here – social and business – and you know, I don't think I'd enjoy Wales if I lived there as much as I enjoy our frequent visits and holidays there, which is our pattern of living at the moment." He was a well-set man with a round face. He was clean shaven, with a tuft of blonde hair amid the black. "Even got the children speaking a little Welsh, just a smattering, but it's a start, so I haven't abandoned my roots."

"So tell me, what's involved?" Hennessey moved and caused the leather of his chair to creak. "I've long been curious."

"Process serving in the main," Daffyd Jones leaned forward, "by which I mean serving writs. Our clients in such cases are firms of solicitors. It basically involves walking up to someone's door and handing them the writ, or just going up to them in a pub and dropping it in their lap. We do some surveillance work for people wanting evidence of this or that; someone wants evidence for a divorce case, or an employer suspects that one of his staff is playing away from home, hobnobbing with the opposition, sometimes it's low-grade infiltration, such as standing all evening in a pub, as close to the till as we can get, to see if the staff aren't skimming money, selling their friends the most expensive lager and ringing the cheapest beer up on the till. That's a popular scam that busy pubs always have to be on the look-out for, particularly in a university city. Bar staff don't see it as theft, but it can cost pubs thousands of pounds a year.

"Any bigger scam though, in a large company, then that's a job for the police rather than a detective agency, because you have to be employed for years before you are let into a huge scam and no private detective will do that.

That sort of deep penetration work is the stuff of fiction.

"We don't do debt recovery and we don't do security work. There's much less violence than you'd think. Hardly any at all compared to police work, despite the impression American films give about PIs. It's also far less glamorous. Why, do you want a job? We do employ recently retired cops, who want to keep their hands in before the allotment or the bowling green beckons."

"You know, you're the second person in the space of an hour to mention my retirement. It's giving me a complex. But no," Hennessey smiled. "No, Daffyd, we want information. Anything you can tell us."

"About?"

"John Cross."

"Oh . . ." Hennessey watched as a scowl fell across Daffyd Jones's face. "Was it Agatha Christie who said that 'the past casts long shadows?' I know what she meant."

"Why does that name ring bells for you?"

"Like the bells of Hell, boy, like the bells of Hell."

Hennessey held eye contact with Jones with a steady stare. "In your own time, Daffyd, in your own time."

"I don't think I saw it at the time." Jones sat back in his chair. "It was only after a few years had elapsed and I was taken out from under his wing . . .

"I was new, needed breaking in, John Cross had some years' service and so we were paired up. John, he had a cult about him, he was a 'coppers' cop'. He was a man who got results, which was all the Great and the Good seemed to want, good-looking statistics. If it looked good on paper, then that was all that was required. I was still in the force when the P.A.C.E. Act came into being and

I remember thinking that that would have sorted Cross out: taped interviews, solicitors present, a responsible adult available in the case of juveniles or vulnerable folk being interviewed. I mean, no more heads being bounced off the wall, no more twisted arms, no more browbeating timid people into confessing to something they didn't do – that's how John Cross worked but nobody saw anything of it unless you were his oppo. I think Cross was one of the reasons I left the force, not *the* reason, but a contributing factor. I'd had enough of the man.

"Why, has someone made a complaint at last? Confess, I'm so very pleased if someone has. I'm prepared to give a statement if someone has, if you want me to. I saw a few things I'm not proud of seeing."

"It might come to that, Daffyd."

"Did you ever meet him?"

"I didn't. Often wished I had for positive reasons, now I'm beginning to feel pleased that I didn't. It seems I was subscribing to the myth, not the man. But I'll make up my mind when I do meet him, if he's still with us, and if he's still *compos mentis*."

"So what's worked itself out of the woodwork?"

"Cornelius Weekes."

Jones shook his head, "That's not a name—"

"Apparent suicide at the beginning of the week, up by Malton way, turned out to be foul play. It got good media coverage."

"Oh yes, the young journalist."

"Freelance fella, he was investigating the case of Charlotte Erickson."

"Oh, the Erickson murder. I was brand new then, Cross was the Investigating Officer, determined to get a result because he'd let the crime get to him. It really annoyed him. You always remember your first cases. Then after a while they all begin to blend and merge, and you have difficulty disentangling one from the other."

"Yes, but you recall the Erickson case?"

"Like I recall yesterday."

Hennessey smiled, although he found time to ponder that very busy folk often have difficulty in remembering what happened 'yesterday'.

"Anything strike you about the case?"

"Much. Particularly John Cross's conviction that the woman Melanie—"

"Clifford."

"That's it . . . Melanie Clifford. He was convinced that she was guilty, and I *mean* as guilty as sin. You see, looking back, I don't think that John Cross was a corrupt officer in the sense that he was open to bribery, and he wasn't criminal. I think that he was a very opinionated person, pathologically so, utterly obsessed with being right all the time about all things, and he just wouldn't see anything that indicated that he was mistaken. He wouldn't ever admit to a mistake. That was the John Cross I recall, and so once he became convinced that Melanie Clifford was guilty, her goose was cooked."

"And you said nothing?"

"I thought he was right. I was white at the knees, remember, he was *the* John Cross, remember? I hadn't paired up with an also-ran, I'd been paired up with a man who could teach me a thing or two about police work, remember? And besides it wasn't John Cross's say so, at the end of the day, it was the decision of the jury in the best and fairest criminal justice system in the world. At the time, when the foreman stood up and said 'guilty', I thought that John Cross must have been right all along. I didn't allow for a lacklustre defence counsel, nor the observed tendency that, once a person stands accused of a crime, especially one that angers the public, including the jury, then much harder work is required to convince a jury of that person's innocence than is required to convince them of that person's guilt."

"That's often because the Crown's case is sufficiently strong, but not always. Anyway, with all the advantages of hindsight, what do you now feel about Melanie Clifford's conviction?"

"A bit unsafe."

"A bit." Hennessey growled. "Only a bit?"

"Well . . . what's she doing these days? Do you know?"

"Getting up at eight o'clock and going to bed again twelve hours later."

"Prison habits die hard, I suppose."

"She's still inside . . ." Hennessey enjoyed watching Jones's jaw sag. "And she's gone blind. Like being in a prison within a prison. Quite sufficient penalty to pay for a conviction that is 'a bit unsafe', don't you think? Especially that it looks increasingly like she was innocent all along. So we're not talking about an unsafe conviction where she did the crime – but the level of proof was insufficient to ensure a safe conviction, we are talking about a monumental miscarriage of justice. And thus far it seems that two people have died trying to prove her innocence."

"Two?"

"Two. As well as Cornelius Weekes, there was also another reporter, about fifteen years ago, who started digging round the same issue, bloke by the name of—" Hennessey turned to Yellich.

"Round." Yellich spoke softly. "Donald Round."

"I see . . ." Jones glanced out of his office window. "Somebody wants the truth concealed." He stood and walked to the window of this office, as if running away from himself, and, thought Hennessey, well he might. Jones put his hand to his brow and brought it down his face and held it over his mouth. "What can I do?"

"You can come back and sit down and tell us all you can remember about the Charlotte Erickson case. We've accessed the file from the void, of course, but it would now seem that it's more akin to a work of fiction."

Jones returned to his seat and sat down heavily. "My life's never going to be the same again."

"Poor you. But if you can, why don't you spare a thought for Melanie Clifford. Her life went bad the moment you knocked on her door one January morning eighteen years ago, and her life won't be the same again. But you might be able to do something that will help her salvage what she can from the years she has left."

"Of course." Jones nodded. "Eighteen years – inside all this time . . ."

"Help us get her out. You see, if she's innocent, then someone else is guilty, that's the thrust of the police stance, not a civil-liberty crusade, but solve one and the other falls into place."

"Yes, I understand that. What can I tell you?"

"Whatever springs to mind. How did it start?"

"As I recall, it was an anonymous phone call, you know, the old classic tip-off."

"What do you know about the call?"

"Male. Adult. That's what the constable at the enquiry desk reported. The details are fresh in my mind because it wasn't just one of my first cases, as I said, it was my first murder case. The phone call tipped us off to the boot of Melanie Clifford's car and the firearm therein, and its connection with murder at Coles Copse Farm near Malton, about which we knew not a dicky bird."

"So what did you do?"

"Followed up the call. Not personally. I wasn't at Melanie Clifford's arrest, I saw her when she was brought in looking very shaken. We phoned the local nick at Malton, they checked the farmhouse, came back very quickly, and told us that a woman's body had been found outside the house, apparently shot in the head."

"So it was a murder enquiry?"

"Yes, right from the start."

"How did John Cross get involved?"

"He wanted the case. He was fifty years old at the time – heavens, he'll be sixty-eight now. He had a good track record, but he wanted to go further. He was a Detective Inspector and that case was his last chance to make Chief Inspector. He wanted it, he wanted it very badly, said as much once. He wanted the promotion and he wanted the enhanced pension that went with it. He knew that if he got a result on the Charlotte Erickson murder, then his promotion was in the bag. And that's what happened. Got the conviction for a high-profile, very nasty murder, got his promotion, left the force at fifty-five with a very nice pension and a mortgage fully paid off."

The phone on Jones' desk rang and he picked it up saying, "No calls, Pauline, I'm in conference." He replaced the phone gently but kept his hand on it for a second or two, then slid his hand off the phone and drew it across his desk top and joined both hands together. "Yes . . . that's how it happened. He wanted the case and the Divisional Commander, a man called Dunlop, let him have it. 'One volunteer is worth ten pressed men' Dunlop said and so John Cross got his case and I was nominated his oppo; 'good learning experience', they said. And it was in a sense, I learned a lot, though I'm not sure that what I learned was what they thought I'd learn."

"Then . . . ?"

"We viewed the corpse – corpse hadn't been moved. Once the police surgeon had certified life extinct, it was left under guard of course."

"Yes . . . yes."

"So we drove out to Malton, and in fact it was during that drive that John Cross said that a result with this case would more or less guarantee his promotion."

"Right, Daffyd, now this is important. Tell me about the corpse?"

"Appearance first, Charlotte Erickson was a blonde woman, very tall, all in proportion, but large boned as well, a bit of an Amazon, I thought. You know, in my life, I've never met a woman who doesn't think there's something wrong with her."

Yellich winced inwardly. The ugliest personality he had ever been involved with, the only involvement which had left him feeling that his life had been contaminated by the experience, had been with a woman who had considered herself to be the image of perfection: the cruelty, the coldness, the naked exploitation of others . . . ugh! But he listened as Jones continued his delivery.

"And I suppose that Charlotte Erickson would have thought herself too large. She'd been dragged there and left face up, a little hole in the front of her forehead. No exit wound. The rifle was a .22. Powerful enough to rearrange

136

the furniture inside her skull but not enough power to blow her head open. Neat job, really, if you're an assassin. She'd been dragged there face up."

"Dragged there, to where she was found, you mean?"

"Yes, she was found in the shrubbery, just to the left of the front door of the house, as you faced the building. There were track marks caused by her body, her heels mainly, in the wet soil. It was a mild winter, no snow, lots of rain, above freezing, so good tracks."

"Any other tracks?"

"A man's boot print."

"As though she had been dragged by a male?"

"Yes," Jones nodded and both Hennessey and Yellich could see that he was hurt by the admission.

"What did Cross have to say about the man's boot print?"

"Nothing. At the time he said nothing, but I know he saw it."

"By that time he would have known about the rifle in Melanie Clifford's car and of her arrest?"

"Yes."

"So the boot print muddied clear waters?"

"Yes."

"This gets worse," Hennessey sighed. "How was she dressed?"

"Indoor clothing. Jeans, T-shirt, trainers."

"Not for out of doors at that time of year then?"

"No."

"Implying that she had been shot indoors?"

"Perhaps, possibly. John Cross didn't seem to be bothered about how she was dressed."

"Doubtless because that would have muddied the waters

even more. Melanie Clifford has always maintained that the house was dark and empty when she arrived. She never went inside the building and Charlotte Erickson never went outside, not alive anyway, otherwise she would have pulled on a coat. No wonder he didn't want to see the male footprint, no wonder he wasn't bothered what the victim was wearing. If he had addressed those issues he would have run the risk of pushing his promotion out of his reach." Hennessey paused. "So then?"

"We interviewed Melanie Clifford."

"So soon?"

"Was a bit premature. I thought John Cross wanted to put the frighteners on her. Really he just let her know that she was in some very hot water and that complete cooperation on her part would be her best option."

"By which he meant a confession?"

"Yes. Then we interviewed Toby Erickson. He drove back down from Edinburgh. He was in quite a state, grief stricken, as you could imagine, recently married."

"He was never in the frame?"

"No . . ." Jones looked at Hennessey and shook his head slowly. "No, cast-iron alibi, you see. Cast iron."

"All right."

"Well, we got the measure of the Erickson operation. Coles Copse Farm used to be a farm but he sold off all the land, except for five acres, to raise money to start a publishing venture – guide books and simplified maps for tourists, that sort of thing. Anyway, Erickson put us on to Melanie Clifford and, looking back, he put us on to her quite quickly. He said that she was spiteful but he didn't think she was capable of murder, 'no, no', he said. He didn't think 'she'd be so spiteful' – those were his words. Told us about their long-term affair: that he'd broken it off after ten years, that he'd left her in her late thirties unlikely to find a husband, that he'd taken up with a younger woman. And though at first Erickson said that Clifford was not malicious enough to kill Charlotte, in the end he told us that she'd become so embittered that the only explanation was that she *had* shot his wife. And John Cross said, 'Yes, I can see that, women can be like that.'"

"He said that?"

"Yes. And I think that it was then that he made up his mind that Melanie Clifford was guilty."

"So then?"

"We returned to York. On the way back John Cross said 'I'm going to break that little bitch', or 'that bitch is going to crack', or something like that. That was his attitude, Melanie Clifford was guilty and that was that. It was just a question of rubber stamping it. We got back to York and Cross just laid into Melanie Clifford, not physically, but verbally, wearing her down, browbeating her. But she didn't crack, she was small but made of strong stuff. Very strong stuff. Eventually he charged her, 'let the Law decide,' he said, 'but I know she's guilty.'"

"Melanie said that she was shown photographs of the deceased?"

"She was. It was John Cross's confrontational attitude, 'look what you've done' attitude."

"She also said that she pointed out the man's footprint at the side of the body?"

"Cross dismissed it. But I did mention it to him and he said, 'It was beforehand', though how he could have known, I don't know but—"

"You were white at the knees, you said."

139

"I was."

"You didn't remain white at the knees forever, though, did you? And you've sat on this for the best part of twenty years."

"And a few other things." Jones glanced down at the carpet. "A few other things as well."

"A few other things, like?"

"Like the pathology report which indicated that Charlotte Erickson was shot by a tall person."

"The flat trajectory? I've accessed the report and reached the same conclusion. She was a tall woman, she would have had to have been shot by someone twelve inches taller than her. Anyone spring to mind, Daffyd?"

"Toby Erickson, who else? The rifle was heavy, had a heavy trigger action. I tested it, no bullets, of course."

"Of course."

"I just couldn't see a small person like Melanie Clifford holding a gun, with careful aim, squeezing the trigger, and getting a perfect dead-centre forehead shot while standing on a chair and aiming on a dark, windy winter's night in January. And not when Charlotte Erickson had conveniently stepped out into that weather wearing a T-shirt and jeans. The whole thing doesn't add up – and deliver." Daffyd Jones leaned forwards and rested his forehead in his hands. "And she's still inside. In that time I've met my wife, married, had children – and all the while she's been doing her bird."

Hennessey and Yellich stood and walked out of Jones' office without saying a word. In the outer office, as they walked past the reception, at which a young blonde woman sat, they heard the intercom click and Jones' musical Welsh accent say, "Pauline, I feel ill, I'm going home. Cancel all my appointments for the rest of the day, will you? Thanks."

*   *   *

"Do you know how far he got?" Yellich sat in the untidy office of the editor of the *Malton Free Press and Journal.*

"Don't, I confess." Horace Clew was a small, bespectacled man, clearly comfortable in a lightweight summer jacket, fawn with glaring pink buttons and, to Yellich's eye, an ill-matching dark blue shirt and tie. "He was doing it off his own bat, as I recall. It's ten – no, more, nearer fifteen years ago. A nice lad, Donald, his death was quite a blow for us, we're quite a small office, as you see."

"Yes, I can see." Yellich looked about him, piles of books and folders seemed to be everywhere, framed photographs of events in Malton's recent history were hung on the plaster walls. The room had a musty smell which Yellich thought appropriate in an odd sort of way. He thought that a musty smell in a Fleet Street newspaper would be highly inappropriate, but the *Malton Free Press and Journal* seemed to belong to a different era, and here, on a summer's afternoon, a musty smell seemed appropriate. "But you do know what he was working on?"

"The questions surrounding the conviction of the person who murdered Charlotte Erickson. He made little secret of it. But as to how far he got, I don't know. I know he visited the woman who was convicted for it – can't remember her name."

"Clifford. Melanie Clifford."

"So it was. Melanie Clifford. Well, he visited her and I also know he visited Charlotte Erickson's family. He once told me privately, in passing, that Toby Erickson was in some way linked to the murder of his wife, but he had an uncrackable alibi, so Donald was thinking along the lines of hired assassins, hit men, so called. Though for myself,

I thought that that was a little fanciful. This is Malton, after all."

"It doesn't mean anything. Organised crime gets everywhere." Yellich's eyes fell on a photograph on Clew's desk, showing a much younger Clew with a child on each knee. "Your children?"

"Yes, up and away now and both of them have become newshounds, the idiots. Do you have children, Mr Yellich?"

"One."

"Nice. Glad we had two, company for each other."

"Yes . . . ours has special needs."

"Oh, I'm sorry."

"Well so were we, when we realised that he wasn't going to be a rocket scientist, then yes, both Sara and I knew great disappointment, but now there's a great sense of privilege. A new world is opening up to us. We've seen things we wouldn't have otherwise seen, and we've made good friends with parents who are in the same position. We've been told that with love, stimulation and support, he could achieve a mental age of twelve by the time he's in his twenties. Then it'll be semi-independent living in a hostel; his own room, a kitchen to cook his own meals if he wants to, but prepared meals if he wants them, and with staff on duty to supervise and advise. We have visited one such hostel with the parents' group, all the facilities are excellent, as is the atmosphere. So when Sara and I get too old to look after Jeremy, we won't worry about where he's going to live if he gets into one of those hostels. It's a real worry off our minds that such places exist."

Horace Clew beamed at Yellich. "I respect your attitude. It's very accepting. I imagine that not all children with your son's—"

"Condition."

"Yes, that's the word. I was going to say 'affliction' but it was clearly inappropriate. Not all children with your son's condition are fortunate enough to have parents with such a healthy attitude."

"They're not, sadly. Our parents' group is composed only of those parents who are interested in their children, and for every parent who is interested in their children, there's two or three who are not. One child with special needs who is accepted by their parents means that two or three are not."

"Pity. Shame on them, I say."

"But we are getting there. One of the aims of the group is to break down prejudice and stigma, to get rid of the 'village idiot' label. But we have digressed."

"Back to Donald Round."

"As you say, Mr Clew. Do you know if he contacted Toby Erickson?"

"I don't. But you're asking the wrong person really, I'm the editor, as I was then, and as I said, this was something he was pursuing in his free time. At the time he was walking out with a girl who worked here as a secretary, Susan Frost by name. I often thought how each was very ill served by their name. Donald was tall and thin and Susan was of such a sunny and warm disposition. Susan was very upset by Donald's death, more than I thought she'd be, so I, so we, found out that they were much more of an item than they let be known. She still lives in Malton, married a solicitor."

"Do you know her address?"

Hennessey took note of the serial number and then held the rifle. He found it to be as Daffyd Jones had observed that morning; heavy, too heavy. The small, finely made

Melanie Clifford wouldn't have been able to hold it with a steady aim. Under the eagle eye of the officer in charge of productions, he worked the bolt action, aimed the rifle at the wall and squeezed the trigger. It was as Jones had also observed, a very heavy trigger action. Hennessey handed the weapon, that eighteen years earlier had been the tool in the hand of Charlotte Erickson's murderer back to the officer in charge of productions. Upon returning to the office, he phoned the collator, recited the serial number of the rifle, and asked him to run it through his "box of tricks".

The children, two boys and a girl, played noisily but good humouredly in the playroom adjacent to the kitchen. Susan Dunwoody, née Frost, laid two mugs of coffee on the breakfast bar – one in front of Yellich – then levered herself on to the stool and sat opposite him. She invited him to help himself to sugar and milk.

"Donald," she sighed. "Oh, Donald . . . I miss him so terribly, he was a lovely, lovely man. My husband, Nigel, he's a good man too, I've done well, I suppose, but, well, a girl has to get married you know, so if you can't be with the one you love, love the one you're with. It makes things easier."

"I'm sorry, I didn't know that you were that close to Mr Round. Mr Clew did indicate it, but only indicated." Yellich sipped his coffee. "I'm sorry if this is difficult for you."

"It isn't easy. But if it's for Donald, then yes, I'll help all I can."

"We know that Mr Round was working on his own investigating the death of Charlotte Erickson . . ."

"Which was the biggest event in Malton in the last one

hundred years. But yes, he was. There's a woman still in prison for her murder."

"We know. We have visited her."

"Donald was convinced that she was innocent."

"We are thinking along those lines now as well, a number of things point to her innocence."

"Took your time, didn't you? I mean nearly twenty years, that's a considerable chunk out of anybody's life."

"Personally, I didn't know a thing about the case until the beginning of this week."

"Sorry . . ." Susan Dunwoody smiled, "I didn't mean to get at you."

"What we want to know is just how far Donald got with his enquiries?" Yellich looked around him. The kitchen was well appointed, with wood trim, and high-tech state-of-the-art appliances. The kitchen window looked out on to a large, well-tended garden at the rear of the house. The house and garden were very much the home of a country solicitor.

A photograph at the end of the breakfast bar showed Susan Dunwoody on her wedding day, and revealed her husband, in a grey suit, to be overweight, bespectacled, balding, and significantly older than his bride, beaming with happiness and clearly delighted with his catch. Clearly, thought Yellich, if there wasn't boundless passion in this union, there was, by means of compensation, much mutual convenience.

"Well, he had visited Melanie Clifford in prison and he had also visited Charlotte's family. Then one evening, we were having a meal out, a rare treat for us. We went to a small bistro in Malton, it's a charity shop now. Donald told me that he thought he'd sniffed round the edge of the story as much as he could and had to talk to Toby Erickson, or to one of the police officers that were involved in the case, or to Melanie Clifford's solicitor. One of those three. The next day at lunchtime he was a bit down in the dumps; he'd contacted all three and, not surprisingly, all three had refused him an interview."

"Hardly surprising the police would speak to him at all."

"He was referred to the police 'press officer'."

"Procedure in such circumstances. He wouldn't get anywhere near the interested officers. Did Donald leave any papers, any notes about his enquiries?"

"Yes. They went up in smoke at the hands of his mother. She was beside herself with grief. She said the notes had brought on his death so . . ."

"I see, of his death, what feelings do you have about it? What information do you have that we might not?"

"Information, nothing. Nothing that you don't have. All I know is what his mother told me and all she knows – knew, she died recently, only half the woman she was before Donald's murder – and she only knew what the police told her. But feelings, feelings, a lot . . . sorry . . . would you care for more coffee?"

Yellich smiled, "No thank you. I'm fine."

Susan Dunwoody said she'd make herself another one, and did so, as if seizing the time to collect her thoughts. Steaming mug of coffee in hand, she levered herself back on to the stool at the breakfast bar and said, "Feelings, inklings, intuition . . ."

"That sort of thing."

"Well, Donald managed to touch a raw nerve, didn't he? It's the only answer, but whose raw nerve? You see Donald wasn't a tough guy, he was bookish, loved justice. No, no he didn't. He hated injustice, that's a little different, hence the determination to do what he could to have Melanie Clifford's conviction overturned, or at least to have her case reopened to force a retrial.

"A few days after that meal, that was our last meal together, he told me that he had received a phone call: someone had information about the case, he said, and wanted to meet him. The rendezvous was a bit difficult for Donald – in the centre of York, late at night, he didn't say where. Anyway, he went. I think he was flushed with excitement that he was going to get his scoop, his 'big one', the one that all cub reporters dream about. And his nature being what it was, he also must have been excited about being on the threshold of doing something big to right a massive injustice, as he saw it. So he went, and didn't come back. His body was found the next morning in one of the snickelways. Donald wouldn't wander into one of the snickelways at night, he just wouldn't. It's my feeling, my belief, that in his excitement about cracking the case, he allowed himself to be lured to his death."

"And would your intuition extend to telling you who lured him?"

"Toby Erickson," she said simply, but with a finality which seemed to echo round the kitchen.

"Do you know him?"

"I know of him. This is Malton, he's one of the local bigwigs, a fat cat who hobnobs with the country set. He remarried after Charlotte was murdered, but that doesn't stop him from having his affairs. He's very good looking you see, and is wearing well. He's very Scandinavian looking; blonde, blue eyes, chiselled features, tall . . . the Vikings were here once, as you know, and they left their mark. We still have waterfalls called 'foss' for example, and they clearly had their way with the Ancient Briton women because their genes still emerge from time to time. You may have noticed as you walk about York or the towns in the Vale – there are lots and lots of short, stocky, dark-haired folk and then, very occasionally, there's a tall, blonde man who just needs a helmet with horns and a double-headed axe to carry off the image. Or there's a flaxen-haired maiden who looks set to drive the livestock up to the high pastures above the fjords for their summer grazing.

"Well, Toby Erickson is one such Viking, even down to his surname. And the women go for him, even though he's pushing fifty, has a wife, children at boarding school, little things like that don't stop Vale maidens throwing themselves at him. Some of them, anyway, and enough to keep him happy."

"You sound bitter."

"I am. As I've just said, Nigel's a good man, and marrying him in the circumstances was the right thing to do, but the fact is that Toby Erickson murdered the only man that I ever loved. But proof . . ." Susan Dunwoody smiled ruefully. "Toby Erickson's too clever to link himself to Donald's murder." She paused. "You know, I may not have amounted to much – only ever a secretary when I was employed – and now I'm a housewife, though I prefer the American term 'homemaker', but that doesn't mean that I'm incapable of adding two and two together. Your sudden interest in Donald's murder: would it be anything to do with the murder of the freelance journalist earlier this week?"

"Yes, it would."

"I knew. I just knew. He had a strange name . . ."

"Cornelius Weekes. He wouldn't have known about Donald's murder, but he lighted on the same story fifteen years on, and probably had got as far as Donald had reached."

"And with the same result."

"Which is why we want to find out how far Donald had got."

"Before a third ambitious young reporter stumbles across the same story?"

"For the sake of justice. Did the police interview you about Donald's murder?"

"Briefly. I remember an elderly police officer, he also interviewed Mr Clew. He didn't ask any penetrating questions. I had the impression it was being done for form's sake. I did tell him about Donald's suspicion about Melanie Clifford's conviction and of his intention to talk to Erickson, and a few others."

"You told him that?"

"Yes – he didn't seem to think it was important."

"Do you recall his name?"

"I don't."

"No matter, it'll be in the file."

"I told him about Donald's going to York to meet someone who had information about Charlotte's death, but Donald didn't know who it was."

"And you told *that* to the police officer as well?"

"Yes. He wasn't interested. He was very perfunctory. It made me angry at the time, but I was young then, early twenties. Now I would have complained that he wasn't trying hard enough. He was old, old for a serving police officer. I understand that in the police you can take your pension at fifty-five?"

"We can."

"Well he was about that, I'd say, looking back, not a lot younger, soft pedalling, coasting to a quiet finish, that sort of attitude. I think he wanted Donald's death to be because he ran into the wrong person at the wrong time. I know that happens, but it just doesn't fit, it doesn't fit Donald's personality. And he was strangled. Did you know that?"

"No . . ." Yellich's voice trailed off.

"The policeman told me that Donald had been assaulted. I assumed he'd been set on and had the life kicked out of him, but at the inquest it was said that he'd been strangled. I mean, that's emotion. You know, that police officer was burnt out, he was a classic burnt-out case, he didn't see anything if it meant work. I only realised that in hindsight. As life went on, I met one or two other men like him, and looking back I now see him for what he was. But it's too late. Or is it? Now you're here . . . perhaps?"

Back at his desk, a freshly made mug of coffee in one hand, Hennessey began to turn the pages of a faded and dusty file on the murder of Donald Round. Interestingly, he thought, interestingly, the interested police officer was John Cross, by then Detective Chief Inspector Cross, and the investigation, Hennessey calculated, must have been the last of Cross's career.

In the last few days, Hennessey had had cause to revise his once high opinion of Cross. He still felt a twinge of disappointment for the man, in that what would have been Cross's last murder investigation should have been unresolved.

The pathologist's report was simple and straight to the point. First of all, there was a head injury which was not in itself fatal – and probably not even sufficient to render the victim unconscious, but which would have been sufficient to disable him – had been delivered to the rear of the skull. An instrument had been used, blunt, akin to a hammer. The victim, Donald Round, aged twenty-seven, had then been strangled. The motive, if there had been a motive, was not robbery; Donald Round's wallet and watch had not been removed. He was found early in the morning by a group of office cleaners as they walked to work, taking their usual shortcut through Mad Alice Lane. The time of death had been estimated to be approximately six hours prior to discovery.

George Hennessey was familiar with Mad Alice Lane; it was, he felt, one of the more pleasing of York's snickelways. It ran a short, narrow course from Swinegate, via a small courtyard, to Lower Petergate, and the name, he had once read, was derived from its most famous resident, Alice Smith, who had lived in the lane when it was called 'Lund's Court' and who was hanged at York Castle in 1825 for the unpardonable sin of being insane.

The scene of crime photographs showed a young man lying face up in a corner of the courtyard. The crime had been committed on a cold, dark night in February. And folk, in Hennessey's experience, do not wander into snickelways at night, even in the summer months, so Hennessey found no difficulty in seeing why Donald Round's body had lain unnoticed for five or six hours in the middle of the city before being chanced upon by a group of office cleaners.

John Cross's neat, exact, just-so handwriting explained how he had interviewed all the deceased's known associates and no one knew of anyone who wanted to harm him, or injure him in any way, and no one could offer any explanation or suggestion as to why he had been in York that night. Cross had concluded that, sadly, Donald Round had been a victim of gratuitous violence. Perhaps, Cross had offered, Donald Round's youthful and bookish appearance meant that he was taken for a student at the university and whose privileged status had rankled a group of miners or farm workers who had had too much beer. And he left it at that.

"But that's just not true, skipper." Yellich spoke softly after he had listened to Hennessey's résumé of John Cross's recording.

Hennessey looked at Yellich and raised an eyebrow.

"I've just come from Susan Dunwoody's home. She was Donald Round's girlfriend at the time and they were very close. She remembers being interviewed by an elderly police officer and she told him about Donald Round's reason for going into York that night. She told him that he was going to meet someone who was offering information about Melanie Clifford's conviction. She told the officer that Donald Round believed Melanie Clifford to have been the victim of a miscarriage of justice and he was trying to expose it. So he knew, skipper. John Cross knew why Donald Round had gone to York that night."

A pause. A silence. An angry fly buzzed against the window frame.

"So why would he falsify his recording?" Hennessey glanced out of the window at sun-baked grey stone buildings, and saw a heat haze rising from the darker roof tiles, all under a blue sky. "He'd got the promotion he wanted after Melanie Clifford's conviction. Why risk blowing his pension just a few weeks or months before his retirement by doing something as foolish and easily discoverable as falsifying his recording?"

"Beats me boss, it's a recklessly stupid thing to do, for any police officer, but so close to retiring. He could have blown everything he worked for. Perhaps Susan Dunwoody was right, maybe he was just a burnt-out case by then."

"A what!"

"A burnt-out case. He just stopped seeing work that had to be done."

"That's the second time today that somebody has used that phrase to me. Commander Sharkey wants me to police a desk until I collect my pension. He had an experience once; I'll tell you the story some time, and he doesn't want any of his staff stiffening due to overwork shortly before they retire."

"Can't see you policing a desk, skipper."

"It won't happen – it won't happen, ever. But let's not jump to conclusions as to why John Cross falsified his recording. I accept that arriving at the conclusion too quickly that there is no work to be done, and believing in your conclusion, is a classic symptom of burn out – but there's another explanation for John Cross's actions."

"That he didn't want anybody to know what Donald Round was working on? To conceal a motive for his murder suited John Cross, it kept the lid on the Charlotte Erickson murder, kept it done and dusted."

"Yes," Hennessey nodded. "It would be difficult for a man like John Cross to accept that he had made a mistake. His self-righteous attitude, as I recall it, meant that he wouldn't be able to handle being exposed as having made a mistake as catastrophic as Melanie Clifford's conviction now appears to have been. I mean, why wouldn't John Cross want to see the safety of Melanie Clifford's conviction being questioned unless he knew that it was suspect?"

"Why else indeed, skipper. Solemn. Very solemn. A right can of worms."

"I won't sleep well tonight, Yellich. I won't sleep well at all."

Six

*In which a simple but ingenious method of confusing
the calculation as to the time of death is described, the
prime suspect is met, and the gracious reader views the
further delights and demons of George Hennessey's
private life.*

FRIDAY

Hennessey and Yellich arrived at Micklegate Bar Police
Station within a few seconds of each other, parking
their cars side by side in the small car park at the rear of
the police station and then walking together towards the
building with Yellich just half a step behind Hennessey.

"It'll be a record." Hennessey pushed open the rear 'staff
only' door of the building and held it open for Yellich.
"After you, Sergeant."

"Thanks, skipper." Yellich stepped over the threshold.
"What will be a record?"

"I was thinking last night; it occurred to me somewhere
between Fredericksburg and Gettysburg . . ."

"Where?"

"I was reading a short volume of the American Civil
War, the author doesn't waste a word and packs it with

detail. But I was between Fredericksburg and Gettysburg and it occurred to me, when I was taking a break from the book, that if we pull this off it'll be something of a record, solving a murder eighteen years after the event. If the first twenty-four hours of any murder investigation, that is the twenty-four hours after the event, is the most important, well it gives you some idea of the obstacle presented by an eighteen-year time gap."

"Aye." Yellich walked with Hennessey down the narrow corridor. "It'll be a dark day for the North Yorkshire Police as well. I could only think of Melanie Clifford last night."

"That's not lost on me either, Yellich."

"You know, skipper, I want to solve the Charlotte Erickson murder, and the Round and Weekes murders too, but part of me wishes they hadn't poked their noses in, part of me would just rather not have found out about this."

"That just makes you human, Yellich."

The two officers signed in at the enquiry desk.

"Lady to see you, sir." The duty constable took the clipboard and timesheet from Hennessey and made a gesture towards the public waiting area.

Hennessey and Yellich turned. Mrs Bailey or Piggot of 3, The Fold, Malton, paramour of the late David Piggot – who a few years earlier had been crushed beneath the wheels of a lorry in Piccadilly – sat on a wooden bench staring blankly at Hennessey and Yellich. Hennessey turned to Yellich. "Nip out and buy some cigarettes and a box of matches will you, please? I think we'll find them useful."

In the interview room, Pauline Bailey snatched at the cigarette offered by Hennessey and held it with quivering fingers to her mouth whilst Hennessey struck the match. She drew deeply on the nail and then sat back in the chair, exhaling through her nose. She was ruddy faced with bloodshot eyes, and was 'humming' for want of a bath and clean clothing. If she did receive her social security allowance the day before there was, Hennessey thought, little doubt as to how she'd disposed of it.

"I remembered something, a couple of things."

Hennessey and Yellich remained silent.

"Only Jasper . . . he's a big dog . . . he gets hungry."

Hennessey took his wallet out, removed a five pound note, which he placed on the table.

"That won't keep him." But she put a grimy, fleshy hand on it anyway.

"There's more where that came from, depending on what you can tell us."

"I had a drink last night, to give myself the courage to get here."

"Just tell us what else you have remembered." Hennessey wore a serious expression, as did Yellich.

"I remembered what else Davy said he did for Erickson. He told me what he put in the boot of the car that night."

"Which was?"

"A rifle."

After a pause, after a silence which spoke of both anger and relief, Hennessey said, "Go on."

"Well that's it. That's what he said he put in the boot of the car. He also said that Mrs Erickson was already dead."

"Sorry."

"She was already dead. I mean before that night – she was already dead."

"She wasn't shot that night?"

"That's what Davy said."

"All right, just take your time, Mrs Bailey, don't get flustered."

"You can call me Pauline. I like being called by my first name."

"Pauline," Hennessey repeated the name, "we've got all the time in the world. So, in your own words."

"That's why Davy did what he did and went and topped himself. He was a good man, thought about right and wrong and such alike, and he couldn't live with himself, so he topped himself."

"And you? You've kept it to yourself all these years?"

"I didn't know how to bring it out, and it was so big. I felt it had better stay hidden. Stupid, I know."

"Is one way of putting it, even though an innocent person has been in prison all this time."

Pauline Bailey began to fight back tears and Hennessey began to feel a certain sympathy for her: she was a child inside, and the world must have been a big and confusing place for her. Her social contacts were limited and her contact with authority was confined to signing herself as 'available for employment' once per week. Added to that was a tendency among humans that Hennessey had encountered before, which was to keep awful truths deeply hidden as a means of coping with them. Putting those things together, Hennessey could see why Pauline Bailey had kept quiet all these years, and he further thought that coming forward like this was, for her, a difficult and courageous thing to do.

"So," he said, "in your own time."

"Davy said she'd been dead for a week."

Hennessey and Yellich glanced at each other and both felt the same sense of disappointment, for now Pauline Bailey was fantasising.

"She'd been shot only twelve hours earlier, Pauline, perhaps a bit more than that, but not much more. We still have the medical report. The state that the body was in was such that it showed death to have occurred within a few hours of being found. So I don't know what Davy said to you but it's not possible for Charlotte to have been shot one week earlier. Now, we're interested in the rifle."

"She was frozen." Pauline Bailey spoke softly and held a steady eye contact with Hennessey.

Hennessey relaxed back in his chair. "Tell me."

"Erickson shot Charlotte one week earlier. You see, he buys food in bulk and he had a huge deep freeze, the type they use in hospitals and hotels Davy said it was big enough to hold a human body. Davy said Erickson shot her and laid her flat in the deep freeze. Took her out two days before she was found. That allowed her body to thaw and made it look like she'd been dead for only a few hours, Davy said."

Again Hennessey and Yellich glanced at each other. "We can only take expert advice on that, skipper," Yellich said softly. "But it might well be possible."

Hennessey turned to Pauline Bailey. "All right, we'll stay with that, we'll have to get expert advice as Sergeant Yellich has just said, but for the moment we'll go along with it. For the moment. Now, why did Davy allow himself to be part of this?"

"Erickson had some sort of hold over him. Exactly what, I didn't know. But Davy said it was like having a gun held to his head."

"This is beginning to sound very interesting." Hennessey offered Pauline Bailey another cigarette which she ignited with the glowing tip of the first nail. "It sheds light, but it doesn't shed evidence. It's what we call hearsay."

"Davy's not around any more, you mean?"

"Yes. That's exactly what we mean. But nonetheless, light is shed."

"The other guy might still be alive."

"What other guy?"

"The other guy who was employed by Erickson, alongside Davy. He was the guy that put the body where it was found." Hennessey put his hand to his forehead. He had the twin urges to hug and to hit Pauline Bailey, but both urges being equal and opposite, they cancelled each other out and did so rapidly. "The name of the other guy?"

"Will something . . . William Pace, Peace, Pierce, that was it, Will Pierce, another lad about Davy's age, about twenty at the time. He'll be pushing forty now."

"If he's still with us."

"Aye . . ." Pauline Bailey drew deeply on the cigarette. "But the way Davy talked about Will Pierce – well I got the impression that Davy was frightened of him, he was something of a hard case was Will Pierce. He didn't seem to be the sort of bloke who'd be bothered about what he'd done, not like my Davy. Davy used to pretend to be hard but he was a lump of putty, really." She paused. "I can't think of anything else to tell you."

Hennessey took a twenty pound note from his wallet and handed it to Pauline Bailey. "That's for Jasper."

"Yes." She snatched the note, "for food, for Jasper."

"And if you do remember anything else."

"Oh, I'll contact you." Pauline Bailey stood hurriedly, knocking the chair back as she did so, clutching the twenty pound note, as if in a great rush to leave the police station.

Hennessey and Yellich looked at each other. Hennessey

tapped the piece of paper in his hand. "It gets worse," he said.

Yellich didn't reply but felt deeply uncomfortable.

"I'm going to have to take this to the Commander. It's now getting to be more a question of what John Cross did do, not what he didn't do." Hennessey glanced at his watch, eleven thirty a.m. "I'll catch him now, before he goes for his lunch. He probably won't thank me for it, it'll ruin his appetite, but he's got to know."

"Anything you want me to do, skipper?"

"Yes, yes, you can ask the collator if we know William Pierce, he'll be in his late thirties now, that's all we know about him."

"Very good, skipper. I can also phone Dr D'Acre. I'll ask her about whether the body could have been frozen and then thawed out."

"No, no, I'd like to do that, Yellich. Rendezvous in my office after lunch. We're going to call on Toby Erickson."

"You look worried, George."

"I am, sir. More on John Cross I'm afraid." Hennessey sat as invited, clutching a piece of paper.

"More indication of a wrongful conviction?"

"In one, sir. We have found another case of a reporter – Donald Round – who was also investigating the Charlotte Erickson murder and who was also murdered."

"Another?"

"Fifteen years earlier. The investigating officer in that case was John Cross."

"Go on."

"Well, John didn't mention in his recording that Donald Round was investigating the murder of Charlotte Erickson, even when he'd been told by the murdered man's girlfriend that Round had gone into York on the night of his death to meet someone who was offering information about the case."

"We don't know who?"

"No, sir. Up until ten minutes ago, I thought John just hadn't any steam left, the burnt-out case that you have mentioned, that he'd reached the stage wherein he was finding reasons, whether he was aware of it or not, for not doing any work."

"About which we have spoken, in another context, as you have said."

"Yes, sir. But now I find this." Hennessey handed Commander Sharkey the piece of paper.

"It's from the collator, as you see. Found it in my pigeonhole a few minutes ago. The rifle used in the murder of Charlotte Erickson is still in productions."

"As it would be, and you have clearly asked the collator to run a check on the serial number."

"Yes, sir. As you see, the serial number wasn't removed by the felon, and it's one of a number of items that were reported stolen in a burglary at Toby Erickson's house a few weeks before the murder."

"Oh."

"Is what I thought, sir. It links Toby Erickson to his wife's murder. It's not a direct link, it's not the unbroken evidential chain that the CPS would want, but it's a link. Checking if the weapon was known to the police would be elementary for someone like John Cross. I cannot believe that he failed to do it."

"But you can believe he chose to ignore his findings?"

"I'm afraid so, sir." Hennessey glanced out of the window of Sharkey's office at a group of tourists walking the walls, 'oh happy they', he thought. "You see, sir, when I first began to doubt the safety of Melanie Clifford's conviction, I thought it must have been down to John Cross' 'tunnel vision thinking', I believe it's called. As soon as he believed in Melanie Clifford's guilt, he closed his mind to any other explanation for Charlotte Erickson's murder. He believed he was right, you see, and that for him was the end of the matter."

"And now?"

"Now I think the whole thing has been jacked up a league. He couldn't have failed to clock the serial number of the rifle. He would have found out what I have just found out, by means of making a simple request of the collator. He must have got this information but, instead of acting on it, he chose to repress it."

"I see."

"This is more than a senior police officer being misguided, or lazy, this is a senior police officer perverting the course of justice. It's corruption. It's probably not the financially driven corruption that you fear so much, sir, but it's corruption just the same, a moral, professional corruption."

Sharkey rested his elbows on his desk top with his forearm held vertically, and sank his forehead into the palms of his hands. "It is, isn't it? But only if he checked whether or not we knew of the murder weapon. However, as you say, such a step is elementary. What do you think happened, George?"

"Now, what I think happened is that Toby Erickson shot his wife a week before her body was found."

"A week?"

"We have recently, this morning, acquired hearsay information that Charlotte Erickson was put on ice after she was murdered – iced after she was 'iced', if you see what I mean."

"Is one way of putting it. But is it possible to do that?"

"We were told that the body was taken out of the deep freeze about forty-eight hours before being found so as to thaw, and give the impression that Charlotte had been deceased for a few hours. I have still to check whether that is possible."

"Yes – but if it's possible?"

"If it's possible, and if it's true, it blows Erickson's alibi, and it suggests that the murder was premeditated to the point that Toby Erickson fabricated the burglary of his own house to distance himself from the murder weapon. He shot his wife and then had the gun secreted in Melanie Clifford's car and offered the investigating officer the cock-and-bull story of Melanie Clifford being a scorned woman in love. And John Cross, hungry for promotion when he had only five years' service left to get it, saw in Melanie Clifford an easy prosecution if, and only if, he was selective about what he thought relevant. In fairness to him, I think he probably did believe in her guilt, but went on from there to close his mind – to the point of suppressing evidence which, if not outright proof of her innocence, would still have cast doubt on her guilt and implicated Toby Erickson. Either that or he couldn't admit to having made a mistake."

"Even if an innocent person went down for life?"

"You see, sir, in his own mind, he'd convinced himself of her guilt so he could live with himself."

"Hope you're wrong. Is there a motive for Erickson to have murdered his wife?"

"Unclear as yet, sir, but she was probably in the way. She brought a lot of money with her when she married, but couldn't live up to the image of the businessman's wife: a bit of a flat, lacklustre personality or so we have been led to believe."

"What's your next step?"

"Call on Toby Erickson, and see what we see, find what we find."

Back in his office, George Hennessey telephoned Louise D'Acre at the Department of Pathology in the York City Hospital.

"Hello . . . it's me."

"Yes, Chief Inspector," D'Acre smiled to herself. She knew his voice immediately.

"Sorry, it's just that I have received some more information about the death of Charlotte Erickson," said Hennessey, who felt he'd recently been calling the doctor too often about work-related matters.

"Who?" D'Acre couldn't remember the name.

"Charlotte Erickson – you may remember that I called on you the other day to pick your brains. She's the woman who was shot eighteen years ago."

"Oh, yes. I said that the time of her death could have been pushed back another few hours."

"That's the one. Could the time window be pushed back for another few days – as much as one week?" Hennessey asked.

"Not a chance," said D'Acre firmly.

"What if the body was kept in a frozen state, and then allowed to thaw out a day or two before it was discovered?"

A pause.

"Well, I've never read any papers on that method of confusing or disguising the time of death, and I've certainly never come across it in my experience, but off the record

. . . well, yes, it's possible but it's only possible because it's not impossible. The body would thaw from the outside in . . . so if the pathologist went deeply enough into the corpse, and noted semi-flaccid skin on the outside, but deep frozen inner lung tissue too, then he'd know at once that he, or she, was dealing with a thawing corpse. But Chief Inspector, medicine is like any other walk of life – there are good doctors and there are bad doctors, just as there are bad and good police officers. And frankly any post-mortem findings are only as accurate as the pathologist dictates them to be."

"I see, possible then, as you say."

D'Acre reiterated her earlier words. "Yes. But I repeat. I say it's possible because I can't say it's impossible. You see, if the pathologist saw the bullet hole in the middle of Charlotte Erickson's forehead and noted the appearance of a corpse as being about twelve hours old with a rectal temperature which is not, despite its name, a deep body temperature, then yes, he'd content himself with a finding that she'd been shot a few hours earlier. And it would not be unreasonable for him, or her, to leave it at that. A Brownie point would be awarded for going deeper but he wouldn't be marked down for not delving further."

"Understood," said Hennessey, admiring the doctor's clarity.

"Besides which, the focus of a post-mortem is *the* cause of death. There is no scientifically accurate way of determining the time of death. That's just as easily done by the police and the good old Mark I eyeball, as it is by the medical profession. There are just too many variables. Somebody died sometime between the time they were last seen alive and when their body was found is really about as accurate as you can get. And after this length of time—

"She was cremated, anyway," Hennessey pointed out.

"That's that then – all gone up in a puff of smoke, but we couldn't have found anything now, not after eighteen years. But the cause was determined, so it's an accurate PM."

"Well, thank you, shall I see—" But Louise D'Acre had already hung up.

Hennessey replaced the phone and looked up to see Yellich standing, smiling, on the threshold of his office.

"You look like the cat that got the cream, Yellich."

"Found William Pierce, skipper. He's doing a ten stretch in Hull for armed robbery."

"Well, he's not going anywhere for the next day or two, he'll keep."

"He's not going anywhere for another seven years or so. At least."

Hennessey smiled and stood up. "Get your hat on, Yellich. Let's go and meet this Erickson fellow."

Coles Copse Farm stood off the Malton to Pickering Road, beyond Old Malton, close to the village of Whickham. The building clearly dated from the early nineteenth century and was of a complicated design. In Hennessey's eyes, it was needlessly fussy, with a multi-angular roof and turrets and dormers. He mused on how the Victorians loved complexity and hated simplicity, God bless 'em, but they gave much to the world: everything from the McNaughton Rules of Evidence to our railway network and the centres of our greatest cities. So, he thought, we can allow them a house, needlessly fussy in its design.

The house was approached down a straight drive, about quarter of a mile in length, lined with cherry trees, which were now, in early May, in full, splendid, pink blossom. The house itself was surrounded by outbuildings, and set in a landscaped garden of about five acres. Two Mercedes stood in the forecourt at the front of the house: one, the larger of the two, was blue, the other, smaller, was pink – clearly saying 'his and hers'. Beyond, in all directions, was lush pasture of green and yellow, dotted here and there with a small copse.

Yellich halted his Escort behind the rear of the smaller Mercedes, and he and Hennessey got out and walked, under the hot sunshine, to the front door of the house. A polished brass knocker seemed to invite Hennessey to rap it, and he did so. It was opened surprisingly quickly by a woman whom both police officers thought to be in her early thirties. She seemed surprised to see Hennessey and Yellich.

"Oh . . . yes?" she said, clearly alarmed.

"Police." Hennessey and Yellich showed their ID cards.

"Yes?"

"You seem startled?"

"I was expecting . . . I thought you'd be . . . oh, never mind. How can I help you?"

"We'd like to talk to Mr Toby Erickson, if he's at home."

"That's my husband, he's in his study. He's quite busy, can I tell him what it's about?"

"We'd rather you didn't. If you'd just tell him that we're here and that we'd like a word with him?"

"Well . . . you'd . . . er . . . better come in."

Mrs Erickson stepped aside and allowed Hennessey and Yellich to step into the cool interior of the house. Into a wide foyer of black-and-white floor tiles and two settees whose sides and back were held together with cord, and which stood facing each other across a coffee table on which there were copies of *Yorkshire Life* and *Country Living*.

"If you'd just like to wait for a few moments, gentlemen, I'll tell my husband you're here." She turned and walked lightly and silently, gliding almost, wraithlike, out of the foyer through an open darkened doorway, leaving Hennessey and Yellich standing in a very large, still, quiet, but refreshingly cool, room.

Seconds elapsed. Minutes elapsed. No sound. No movement. Either inside or out.

Hennessey and Yellich glanced at each other. Yellich said, "This house has an atmosphere, skipper, and no mistake."

Hennessey nodded. "You know, I think you're right. I'm picking up something as well, not a supernatural presence, but a sense that 'something happened here'."

"That's what I sense, skipper. I've come across it from time to time in my life. You know, you go into a room, nothing moving, nothing out of place, no noise, yet you say to yourself 'something's happened'. I feel that here. Not a recent happening."

"No . . . about eighteen years ago, wouldn't you say?"

Before Yellich could answer, Mrs Erickson, courtesy of soft-soled shoes, glided back into the foyer, a T-shirt and shorts completed her dress. "My husband extends his apologies, he'll be with you directly," she said, sniffily, and then turned and glided away again. Hennessey said, "Thank you," to the retreating figure, though he doubted that Mrs Erickson was much interested in his response.

Then more waiting – waiting to the point of imperious arrogance, Hennessey thought, but said nothing.

Eventually, twenty minutes after Mrs Erickson had assured them that her husband would be with them 'directly', Toby Erickson stepped into the foyer. He said nothing but stared at Hennessey, his head slightly jutting out from his shoulders. Hennessey remained silent, too, but held the stare. Then, when it became clear that the man was going to stand there, statue-like until spoken to, Hennessey said, "I am Chief Inspector Hennessey, North Yorkshire Police, and this is Sergeant Yellich."

As if triggered by action, Erickson stepped forwards, relaxing in his posture, head back in its normal place on his shoulders, smiled, and said, "I am Toby Erickson, how can I help you? Please take a seat."

Hennessey, who so detested game players, felt a surge of dislike for Erickson rising inside him, but contained his feelings and sat, with Yellich, side by side on one of the settees.

Erickson sat opposite them – broad shoulders, casual trousers, sandals, a good head of hair for his fifty years of life – and smiled broadly. "How can I help you gentlemen?"

"Probably you can't," Hennessey replied and, as he did so, he noticed Erickson relax with a slight but perceptible discharge of anxiety which he thought was interesting. Very interesting indeed. For here, he observed, here is a man with a guilty conscience, here is a man with something to hide. But here also is a clever man, a cautious man, a ruthless man. Softly, softly, catchee monkey. "I'm sorry if I'm going to open painful wounds but it's about your wife."

"Erica?" Erickson pointed to the open doorway.

"No, Charlotte." And Hennessey saw Erickson tense again as if he realised his past was catching up with him, and tapping him gently, but menacingly on the shoulder.

"Oh . . . Charlotte . . . yes, a tragedy. She was found just outside in the shrubs beneath the window there. Why the sudden interest? That was nearly twenty years ago . . . it's as if it belongs to another lifetime."

"As it would, I dare say . . . the thing is Mr Erickson, is that a number of disquieting points, or issues relating to her murder have begun to surface."

"Oh . . . I thought the conviction was quite safe. Melanie Clifford shot her, cold blooded – a premeditated murder. That's that."

"Well, you see Mr Erickson, that is not 'that'. It's not 'that' at all."

"What are you saying?" Erickson scowled. Hennessey saw that the man had a short fuse, as well as being cautious. He was the sort of man who was cautious so long as he kept his head. But if he lost his head, he'd trip himself up. That could be very useful indeed.

"It's not so clear cut as we thought at the time. We have to ask a few questions."

"Questions?" Erickson leaned forward, resting his elbows on his knees. "Such as?"

"What exactly was your relationship with Melanie Clifford?"

"We were lovers. She had clerical and secretarial experience which I needed when I was setting up my business."

"Your business?"

"Sommaren Press." Erickson spoke proudly. "Sommaren is Swedish for 'the summer'. It was a name I chose in recognition of my Scandinavian ancestry."

Hennessey couldn't take that away from him: the blonde hair, the blue eyes, the strong, muscular frame, running a little to fat – he was a Nordic in any man's language.

"We can't trace the lineage back as far as we'd like, but

the name, the physical appearance . . . that's the reason I chose the name 'Sommaren'. We publish guide books and simplified maps for tourists. Sold the farm, except five acres, to raise the money to start the venture. Melanie Clifford was there at the beginning, she was working late one winter's night and well, it went from there. So, apart from being rejected in favour of a younger woman, she also felt that she had a share in Sommaren Press, but that, I can tell you, was feverish imagination on her part. She and I were lovers, yes, but an offer of marriage was never made, and she was never anything more that an employee of the company. Being in at the conception of a company doesn't give you a lawful share in it."

"Of course . . . but your relationship. Were you long-term lovers?"

"Ten years. Long term enough."

"Continuously?"

"Yes. Ten years, through thick and thin."

Hennessey held the pause. "You see, she doesn't quite remember it like that."

"Oh . . ." Another scowl. "You've spoken to her?"

"Yes. The day before yesterday. You see, she told us – me and Sergeant Yellich here – that you and she were lovers for about ten years, but that the nature of your affair, your relationship, was that it was on-off, on-off, that you'd drift apart sometimes for long periods of time, and then you'd pick up with each other again. Then after a while you'd drift apart. Benjamin Ffrench, Charlotte's brother—"

"Yes. I know who he is, thank you."

"Well, he confirms that. As does Melanie's family. Benjamin Ffrench also confirms that the offer of marriage was never made because Melanie wouldn't have been able to carry the part of a businessman's wife. 'Out of her social depth', I think he suggested . . . whatever one's social depth is."

"That's right. You see, no offer of marriage."

"But for us, that means the notion of Melanie Clifford being a scorned woman becomes a little hard to swallow. The motive for her murdering Charlotte Erickson gets weaker and weaker. She, in fact, tells us she sent you a card congratulating you on your engagement."

" 'Well, she would, wouldn't she?' to paraphrase a famous retort during a famous trial. She's trying to throw you off the scent, laying a false trail. That's why I was very impressed by the police officer who handled the case, Mr Cross. He was angry about a young life being taken, and taken out of spite and vindictiveness. He saw Melanie Clifford for what she was. He saw her motivation as clear as crystal."

"Ah, well, Mr Erickson, there's the problem in a nutshell. Have you looked at crystal? It isn't really very clear."

"What are you saying?" Erickson clenched his fist.

"Did you benefit from your wife's death?"

"Benefit? We were only six months married."

"Just answer the question."

"What are you driving at?"

"We have reason to believe that your business was struggling when you married, and that upon marriage Charlotte brought a lot of money to your finances."

"There's no denying that. Though while the company was struggling, you shouldn't infer from that that the company was close to folding. I'm confident that we would have pulled through without the money that Charlotte brought with her, but yes, the money was useful. Mind you, what company wouldn't refuse a massive injection of cash, that's what it's all about, isn't it?" Erickson smiled. "So, don't read too much into it."

"So you have remarried?"

"As you have seen, happily, we cope with the age difference, two children at school, they make us happier."

"I can imagine."

"You know, I wish you people would let things lie down and die. There's nothing to beaver away at. I can cope with reporters looking for a story. But when the police, who are always bleating about lack of resources, start digging up a long-buried case that should be left to rest in peace—"

"Reporters?"

"Three all told. Over the years."

"Three?"

Yes, one fellow a few years after the murder. I refused him an interview, never heard from him again, then the man who was murdered earlier this week. Weekes? Was that his name?"

"Yes."

"Then just yesterday a woman phoned, said she was researching the murder of Charlotte Erickson for a magazine article . . . I gave her a bit of a mouthful and put the phone down on her."

"Did she give a name?"

"Probably, but I took no notice of it. I wasn't going to speak to her any more than I was going to speak to Weekes or the other guy. I mean, what right do they have to pry into my affairs, and my grief for that matter. None, have they? None."

"What specifically was the slant of the third reporter's questions?"

"Well, she didn't get very far but from what I could tell,

she thought Melanie Clifford's conviction was unsafe – now that, let me tell you, is one safe conviction, she even lost the appeal. How safe can you get?"

"Mr Erickson, where were you on Sunday last, say from Sunday midnight to Sunday at ten a.m.?"

"In Venice."

"Venice? Italy?"

"Well, the only other Venice I know is in San Francisco, but yes, the Italian Venice, *the* Venice. Erica and I took a weekend break. Flew out on Friday, returned on Monday of this week. We have documentary evidence: hotel receipts, travel documents, photographs any day now, and the airline will have our names on the passenger manifest. We flew British Midland from Leeds/Bradford and returned to Leeds/Bradford."

"So you were not in the country at all!" Hennessey gasped.

"No. Why?"

"Nothing."

"Oh . . ." Erickson leaned back and smiled, "I think I now see how your little brain is working, Chief Inspector. This isn't about Charlotte's murder . . . it's about the murder of Cornelius Weekes, whose murder I read about in the *Yorkshire Post*, and also heard about on the regional news. I recognised him at once as the fella who was seeking an interview, and now you want to know where I was when he was murdered? So I'm a suspect, am I? Well, sorry to disappoint you, gentlemen – I have a cast-iron alibi."

"Which we will check for form's sake," Hennessey said but he felt the loss of a promising line of enquiry.

"Oh do, do check it."

"I don't suppose you know where you were on the night of February the twenty second, three years after Charlotte's murder?"

"Fifteen years ago? That's a tall order isn't it?" But Erickson was smiling.

"It's a long shot, but they've paid off before."

"And it'll pay off now." Erickson stood. "Please wait here." He walked away as if determined to prove something.

Hennessey turned to Yellich. "Now that has muddied the waters."

"Hasn't it just, skipper, hasn't it just."

"If Weekes and Round were murdered for reasons other than anything to do with Charlotte Erickson's murder, then we've been looking in the wrong place all along."

"Not entirely fruitless though, skipper, I mean, we've heard enough this week to make me very unhappy about Melanie Clifford's conviction. We can't sit on that – it's a bit like finding Zerzura."

"Finding what?"

"Zerzura," Yellich repeated. "It's a Bedouin legend, the lost city of Zerzura, made of gold, somewhere in the desert, but you never find it if you look for it. You only find it if you're close to giving up the search for something else but find one last ounce of effort. Such as an Arab who is searching for a lost camel and is about to give up, but finds the strength to look over one last dune . . . it's then that he stumbles upon Zerzura – and his fortune, measured in untold wealth. This week we started looking for the murderer of Cornelius Weekes, and in the process we have apparently stumbled across two more unsolved murders, and an unsafe conviction. Zerzura."

"Well, all we need now is the untold wealth."

Erickson returned looking triumphant. "I've always kept my business diaries." He held up a desk diary. "So," he said, sifting through to find the dates, "February the twenty second . . . there you are." He turned the diary round and handed it to Hennessey.

The entry for that date read 'West Country Tours, Bristol, Smith's Hotel' the following day read 'Historical Tours, Antwerp Place TCR – ten a.m.' Hennessey handed the diary to Yellich who read the dates and then handed the diary back to Erickson.

"I remember those two days. I drove down to Bristol on the twenty second, spent the night in a hotel in the city. I had a lady friend with me. The next day we drove to London and I did business with another coach tour operator, both wanted maps and guide books for their tours. TCR is short for Tottenham Court Road. They may still have documentary evidence to confirm my presence there, something else you can check for form's sake. I returned to Yorkshire in the evening of the twenty third. I'm still in contact with the lady in question, the lady who accompanied me on the trip. There's nothing between us any more, and she's married herself now, but if you're discreet, she'll confirm what I have told you."

"If you don't mind."

Erickson gave a name and an address in York and Yellich noted it on his pad.

"Why?" Erickson asked as Yellich folded his pad. "What happened on the twenty-second of February that year, that you should question me about my whereabouts?"

"Donald Round was murdered in Mad Alice Lane in York."

"Who's he?"

"The first reporter to ask you for an interview about your first wife's murder."

"Well, I never. So that's why I didn't hear from him again. And all along I thought it was my forceful personality that put him right about the importance of privacy and the wrongfulness of meddling. But he was murdered too . . . well, well, well."

"Both enquiring about Charlotte Erickson's murder, both murdered shortly after contacting you. You can perhaps understand our wish to establish your whereabouts on the night of both murders."

"I can. I'm not happy, though, that you could even think for one second that I had anything to do with either murder, but at least I'm going to be eliminated from your list of suspects, or am I?"

"If your alibis check out, you'll be eliminated."

"Well, thank God for that. Now if you'll excuse me . . ."

"Not quite yet, Mr Erickson."

Erickson's face set hard. "What now?"

"Davy Piggot, William Pierce."

"What of them?"

"So you know them?"

"Names from the distant past. Two lads I employed to do odd jobs, manual labouring, just to get on top of the five acres that I retained when I sold off the farm. I wanted a garden for the house."

"Five acres . . . that's a generous garden."

"No other employment for them?"

"No. Nothing." Erickson clenched his fist.

"We'd like to take a look at the outbuildings."

"Would you?"

"Yes, yes, we would." Hennessey spoke softly. "We don't have a warrant, but should one be necessary—"

"And if I refuse to let you look inside the outbuildings?"

"Well, that's when a warrant would be necessary. To be blunt, Mr Erickson, we're going to look inside the outbuildings with or without your cooperation, but we're going to look inside them."

Erickson shrugged. "Be my guest. I've nothing to hide."

"Thanks, then we will. Particularly the outbuilding that contains the deep freeze."

Erickson paled, his jaw slackened, he gaped at Hennessey who felt the man's reaction to be pleasing – oh yes, most pleasing, passing pleasing. He had clearly touched a raw nerve, and beside him he sensed that Yellich, too, had picked up the significance of Erickson's expression.

"You see, Mr Erickson," Hennessey decided to press the advantage, "I'll explain to you why we're keen to talk to you about the murder of your first wife. There are a number of points that were not introduced during her trial, nor at the appeal, and which seem to point the finger of suspicion away from Melanie Clifford. And if she has been wrongfully convicted, we want to find the real culprit."

"Points? Such as?"

"The fact that the murder weapon was reported as being stolen from your house a few weeks prior to your wife's murder."

"I was burgled . . . yes, how did you know it was the same gun?"

"The serial number."

Erickson gasped, made as if to say something, then checked himself. But he could not, in Hennessey's eyes, prevent himself from looking very uncomfortable.

"It links you with the murder."

"It links me with nothing. How can I be responsible for a gun's use once it has been stolen from me?"

"If it was stolen."

"What are you suggesting?"

"That it's the easiest thing in the world to fabricate a burglary. People do it all the time for the insurance money. Then there are Davy Piggot's prints on the boot of Melanie Clifford's car, just where someone would hold the boot when taking something out, or putting something in. At the time he wasn't known to us, so we didn't have his prints on file, and we probably didn't know that he was employed by you at the time so we wouldn't have taken his prints. But now we find out that he was employed by you, contemporary with your wife's murder. It lends credence to Melanie Clifford's claim that the rifle was planted in her car."

"All right, it lends credence, but it proves nothing. The woman was seething with hatred for Charlotte."

"So you say, Ms Clifford says different." Hennessey held eye contact. "Unfortunately Davy Piggot is no longer with us."

Erickson smiled, as if relieved.

"He was knocked down in York after a drinking session, went under the wheels of a heavy goods vehicle."

"I'm sorry to hear that." But it was not, neither Hennessey nor Yellich felt, said with sincerity.

"The driver said that he appeared to throw himself under the wheels of the lorry and his lady friend told us that he seemed troubled and preoccupied at the time of his possible suicide, as if guilt ridden, but she didn't tell us what about."

"Oh."

"Until this morning."

Erickson said nothing.

"This morning she told us that Davy had confessed to her that he had put a rifle in the boot of Melanie Clifford's car. Unfortunately that's hearsay evidence, can't be used in court."

"How unfortunate."

"But it does tie in with his fingerprints being found on the boot of Ms Clifford's car."

"So what?"

"Davy Piggot also told his lady friend that William Pierce had taken the body from a deep freeze in one of the outbuildings forty-eight hours before it was found, to allow it time to thaw, so that it had a temperature and an appearance which would have been consistent with a corpse being about twelve hours old. Our pathologist tells us that it would be possible to carry off that subterfuge if the post-mortem was insufficiently thorough. If the pathologist determined the cause of death, which was never in doubt, that would be a thorough enough PM to satisfy Home Office criteria. Time of death is never more than a guess, anyway, and scientists hate guessing."

"This is getting preposterous, and it's all still hearsay."

"Which is why we'd like to talk to William Pierce."

"Then all you've got to do is find him. He was a ne'er do well. He left the area. He's probably in Australia now."

"Oh, he's alive all right, and he didn't go as far as Australia. He made it as far as Hull, where the English Civil War started when the people refused to let the King enter the city 'Because he wanted to take—'"

"—weapons from the armoury. Yes, I grew up in Yorkshire too."

"Actually I'm a Londoner," Hennessey said, "but William Pierce is in Hull, HM Prison, to be exact. Very accessible for us. What is he going to tell us, do you think?"

"I have no idea. I refuse to answer any more questions without a solicitor being present. Now, do you want to see the outbuildings or not?"

"No." Hennessey stood, Yellich did likewise. "After eighteen years there wouldn't be a lot of purpose. But thank you for your cooperation."

"A lot of progress there, skipper. That's a man with something huge to hide."

"Two steps forward and one back." Hennessey sat in the front passenger seat. "In fact I'm not sure if we are any further forward. His alibis for the murders of Cornelius Weekes and Donald Round appear sound, both easily checked. So easily checked that they will be sound. And we're really no nearer to linking him to the murder of Charlotte Erickson. And now pressure is on us because of yet another reporter that's picked up the story."

"Yes . . . I forgot about her." Yellich kept his eyes on the road. "We must find out who she is. She's in danger."

"Mortal danger," Hennessey said as a motorcyclist overtook them, a young man who drove his machine by leaning low down over the handlebars to reduce the wind drag caused by his body. Hennessey watched the motorcyclist and winced inwardly. Only a few weeks to go now, a matter of days, before the awful anniversary; the dreaded and dreadful thirteenth of June. That was the date when, as a young boy of about eight years of age, he had lain awake in his room in his parent's terraced house on Colomb Street, Greenwich, at the bottom end of Trafalgar Road, and had listened as his beloved elder brother had driven off on his beloved Norton. George Hennessey had lain in his bed straining his ears to catch every last fading decibel as Graham rode westwards towards the Maritime Museum and the Naval Academy, the sound eventually being drowned by a drunken Irishman walking beneath his window chanting his Hail Mary's.

Then later, there was a knock on the front door. The young Hennessey heard urgent voices and his mother wailing as only an inconsolable mother could wail. He remembers his father sitting on his bed, struggling to tell him that Graham would not be coming home, and doing so in such a way that an eight-year-old could understand, managing only to say that Graham had ridden "to Heaven . . . ahead of us . . . to save a place for us".

Then there had been the funeral, an awful summer's funeral. Graham's coffin was lowered into the ground in the sort of weather that would normally have him polishing his machine, or taking 'young George' for a spin round Blackheath Common, or across Westminster Bridge and back across Tower Bridge: that ride, Hennessey recalled, was his favourite. After that, he had tried to lead a normal life. But each day he sensed a very real void, in which there should have been someone for him to follow.

And now, sitting in the passenger seat of Yellich's car, and watching the yellow machine speeding away down the pasty grey road between the lush green foliage, he again understood his reluctance to drive at all during his lifetime, from that awful day to this. He could never fathom humankind's love affair with the most dangerous machine ever invented – whether two wheels or four.

*   *   *

That evening, after a supper of wholesome casserole, and after walking Oscar, Hennessey stood in the back garden, in the orchard, close to the 'going forth' and sipped a mug of tea. He said, "I just want you to be pleased for me, dear heart, my feelings for you haven't diminished . . . on the contrary, they get stronger by the day, but she answers something, some deep need and I answer something in her, it's mutual. She knows all about you – I want you to be pleased for us." And then, as happened on earlier occasions, he had felt a glow of a warmth which couldn't be explained by the setting sun, and seemed to come from all around him, from where Jennifer's ashes had been scattered.

He ensured that Oscar had a substantial amount of food, and a lot of water, and then packed an overnight bag. He drove to Easingwold, to a half-timbered house with a gravel drive. He knocked on the door which was opened by a slender, smiling woman in her forties. They held and kissed each other. Hennessey peeled off his jacket and hung it on a peg in the hall. He walked into the kitchen, a hive of activity wherein riding equipment was being polished and buffed for the 'event' the following day. Diane was the only offspring absent – she was at the stables, brushing Danny. Hennessey, upon invitation, sat next to Daniel, the other 'Danny' in the household and together they demolished his maths homework.

Later that evening he sat at the table opposite the slender lady who had warmly opened the door to him. As they listened, Fiona, Diane and Daniel shifted themselves to bed with much running up and down the landing and fighting for the use of their bathroom – the house having two, one for the children, and the other designated for adult use only. Then silence descended.

"Well," he smiled, "shall we go up?"

"Yes." Louise D'Acre returned the smile. "Yes."

Seven

In which the resolution to all three murders is reached, although the gentle reader may feel George Hennessey's frustration on the one hand and his deep dismay upon the other.

SATURDAY

P rogeria.
    That was the word which came rapidly to Hennessey's mind. He had driven, alone, to meet John Cross in his house in Wetherby. He found John Cross's house to be meticulous with a neatly kept garden, hardly a blade of grass, it seemed, was out of place. John Cross's car was similarly well looked after, carefully polished – and parked perfectly on the driveway – with badges of motoring organisations bolted to the front bumper with millimetre-measured precision between each one. The whole image spoke to Hennessey of a man who would not know the meaning of the word latitude. For this man the world was composed of black or white, of right or wrong, of good or bad: there was no in-between.

    Hennessey got out of his car, walked up the drive and knocked gently on the front door. It was opened timidly by a frail, silver-haired lady who said "Yes?" through the small crack she allowed between the door and the doorframe. Before Hennessey could answer, a powerful male voice from inside the house bellowed "Who is it, woman?" Hennessey said his name and that he'd like to speak to John Cross, to which the lady turned and said, "It's somebody for you." The lady pushed the door to, but not shut. She seemed to retreat, then there was the sound of a heavy footfall, and Hennessey had the impression of 'woman' as Cross had referred to his wife, being pushed aside. The door was wrenched open and John Cross stood in the doorway looking down, angrily, at Hennessey. It was at that point that the word 'Progeria' came to mind.

Progeria was, so far as Hennessey understood, a horrible but mercifully rare medical condition wherein the human body races through its life span resulting in the sufferer dying effectively of old age when he or she is only a child of about seven or eight years. At death, the child is the size of a normal seven- or eight-year-old, with a seven-or eight-year-old's emotional development, but with mottled, wrinkled skin, arthritis, without teeth and hair and failing internal organs. No cure, you have to live with it. And die with it. The disease came to Hennessey's mind as he was confronted with a towering, glowering John Cross. Because if there was an antithesis to this illness John Cross was blessed with it – for this was not a man who appeared to be in his late seventies. Hennessey had met men in their late fifties or early sixties who did not appear to be as youthful or as physically fit as John Cross. But then, Hennessey thought, that's 'age'. It's a concept, it comes to some earlier than it comes to others, and it had come to John Cross only minimally.

"Yes!" John Cross glared at Hennessey.

"John Cross?"

"Yes."

"Chief Inspector Hennessey, Micklegate Bar Police Station, York."

And instantly John Cross's manner changed. He smiled warmly, "Yes?"

"I wonder if I could have a word with you, sir?"

"John . . . call me John."

"I'd like to pick your brains about one of your old cases."

"If I can remember anything." He stepped aside. "Won't you come in?"

Cross led Hennessey into the living room of his house, pausing as he passed the kitchen door to snap 'tea!' to his wife, who lunged with instantaneous obedience for the kettle.

The living room, like the exterior of the house, was, in Hennessey's view, a further model of intolerance, even to the point that the books on the shelves were arranged in volumes, with the tallest spines at the ends of the shelves and the short-spined volumes in the centre. There wasn't a single book out of place to interrupt the curves thus created. John Cross sat in a chair in the corner from which he could survey the entire room. *His* chair. Hennessey, by contrast, was invited to sit in the chair behind which the door opened.

"How can I help you? I didn't catch your full name."

"Hennessey."

"First name." Snapped, almost shouted.

"Chief Inspector. I'd like to keep this as formal as possible."

"Then you'd better call me Mr Cross." In a louder voice he shouted, "Forget the tea!", which brought the sound of a nervous clatter of cups from the kitchen. "So?" he said icily.

"So . . ." Hennessey collected his thoughts. "You know, it was quite a working week last week."

Cross glared at him.

"Started with an apparent suicide that became a murder, led to another murder, then another murder, and then the issue of a wrongful conviction was added to the pot. Some week, but it's like that occasionally, as I'm sure you'll remember."

"Charlotte Erickson, Melanie Clifford. It's that case that you want to talk about."

"Yes. Why bring it up?"

"Because a woman reporter phoned me this week wanting an interview about the case. She was well out of luck, I won't talk to reporters. And I'm reluctant to talk to you, unless I have to."

"Well, let's keep it off the record for now, see how far we get."

"Clifford was guilty. Look, Chief Inspector, I did well in the police, I retired with the rank I wanted to retire with, and I got there because I got results and I got results by being right. Do you understand? Melanie Clifford murdered Charlotte Erickson. We had the motive, the classic scorned woman and we had the murder weapon in Clifford's car. I mean, what more do you want? It was an open-and-shut case. Anyway, it went before a jury and then a Court of Appeal. So, she went down for a twenty-year minimum – I thought she'd be out in ten, but she'll be up for parole soon. At least she'll be able to breathe free air again, which is more than Charlotte Erickson has been able to do for the last eighteen years. She breathed her last bit of free air when she was twenty-seven years old. You know, I knew what that was like for her family. I had a twin sister . . . she was knocked down and killed by a hit-and-run driver when she was twenty-seven."

"I'm sorry, I didn't know."

"Well, you know now. There was something special between me and Holly, always knew what the other was thinking . . . it's like that with twins. A part of me died when Holly died, and they never found the driver who killed her. So I know what it means to lose someone you love, who is only young. It deserves a penalty."

"It does, but only if the culprit pays."

"The culprit *did* pay. As soon as I saw Melanie Clifford, I knew she was guilty. I just knew it. Don't be fooled by her waif-like appearance . . . she's a funnel-web."

"A what?"

"An Australian spider, small but deadly. Remember, 'The Devil can assume a pleasing form.'"

"Cornelius Weekes would have disagreed with you."

"Yes . . . he wanted an interview, he got refused as well."

"Donald Round didn't think so either."

"Who's he?"

"One of your last cases. He was strangled in Mad Alice Lane."

"Oh yes, I remember – wrong place at the wrong time, such happens."

"But he was also a reporter, also investigating the murder of Charlotte Erickson, also believing in Melanie Clifford's innocence. Links his murder with Cornelius Weekes."

"Maybe – they're a long time separated."

"Possibly. But possibly they were on to something. Possibly somebody didn't, and still doesn't, want something to come out."

"Perhaps, perhaps some things are better left hidden. Perhaps you'd better not go opening Pandora's box. Melanie Clifford will be a free woman in two years' time. Perhaps you ought to leave it at that."

"Are you warning me off?"

"No, I'm not doing anything. Look, just why do you want to talk to me, Chief Inspector?"

"I don't know," Hennessey smiled. He struggled with the question. "And I emphasise that this is off the record. I think I'm here for my own edification, my own curiosity."

"So, I'm indulging you?"

"Yes, yes, you are."

"So long as that's clear."

"But there are some questions I want to ask you about Charlotte Erickson's murder."

"Go on," Cross growled slowly.

"Who first pointed the finger at Melanie Clifford?"

"Anonymous phone call about the location of the body and the murder weapon, then the deceased's husband provided us with the motivation, the case was closed a few hours after it was opened."

"And you were happy with that?"

"Of course. It was as neat as neat could be. Why dig deeper?"

Hennessey groaned. "Were you tired at the time? I don't mean sleepy, I mean emotionally speaking."

"I don't recall."

"But something stopped you digging deeper?"

"Logic. There was no need."

"You didn't fingerprint Erickson's employees at the farm?"

"He didn't have any. He had business premises, but no one worked at the farm."

"He had two. Two young men, Pierce and Piggot. If you had asked about the other people in the house, you would have found out about them. Piggot's prints were on the boot of Melanie Clifford's car. Piggot committed suicide, but not before he confessed to his lady friend that he had placed the rifle in Melanie Clifford's car."

John Cross's jaw sagged, slightly.

"And there was the footprint, by the body. Male footprint, heel down, just as it would be as if it were left by a man dragging the corpse of Charlotte Erickson."

"And which was probably there for days. You're contaminating the crime scene."

"And the rifle. Where did that come from?"

"I've no idea."

"Haven't you?" It was Hennessey's turn to growl. "Did you do elementary checks?"

"Of course."

"Sadly in your case, Mr Cross, it's not an 'of course' question. If you had done elementary checks, you would have found that the rifle was reported stolen from the Erickson household a few weeks before Charlotte Erickson's murder."

Cross remained impassive.

"So you either did the checks, found something that would have involved deeper investigation, or you didn't do the checks at all and proceeded to a speedy conclusion. One or the other, but either way, you didn't need promotion when you were investigating that case, you needed retirement."

"I think I'd like you to leave my house." Cross flushed with rage.

Hennessey stood. "I think I'd like to leave too. But tell me something, how was it that the bullet entered Charlotte Erickson's head with a flat trajectory if Melanie Clifford was eighteen inches shorter than Charlotte Erickson? And don't say she stood on a stool to do it, on a dark winter's night."

"Get out!"

Hennessey walked down John Cross's drive towards his car. Cross stood on the threshold of his house, calling after Hennessey, "I was right, I was right, I was right."

Driving away, Hennessey could only fear for the safety of the timid Mrs Cross, trapped in a small 'just so' house with her furious, mad tiger of a husband.

George Hennessey finished work that Saturday at two p.m., drove home and passed a quiet afternoon sitting in a canvas chair on the patio at the back of his house reading a compendium called *Great Military Blunders* and glancing up occasionally to watch Oscar exploring the shaded areas of the garden. Later that day he drove out to Skelton to the warmth of Louise D'Acre and her household. It was unusual for D'Acre and him to spend two consecutive nights together – pleasantly though, he thought, pleasantly unusual. Sunday was also a quiet day; unimportant administration at work, a quiet evening at home, a walk with Oscar and then a walk, alone, into Easingwold for a glass of stout.

After a morning shift devoted to paperwork, Yellich returned home whereupon he and his wife and son spent the afternoon walking near Grassington. Physical stimulation and a sense of achievement was just as important for Jeremy's development as emotional and intellectual stimulation, so said the clinic, and a hike in the country was ideal. Such walks were a regular feature of the York District Learning Difficulties Group. Sometimes there were group rambles and sometimes, as on this occasion, they were just the parents and child.

MONDAY

"I want to deal." He was a hard man, Hennessey saw that. So did Yellich. Thirties, muscular, a scar on his cheek, missing teeth, tattooed and cold, piercing eyes. A desperate, desperate animal inside the blue shirt and blue jeans of an inmate in HM Prison, Hull. A man for whom survival had become an issue. "I'm three into a ten stretch for armed robbery. Everybody knows you can't do ten years in maximum security and still have a mind left at the end of it. I haven't exactly cooperated, if you see what I mean . . . I want something to take to the parole board."

Hennessey looked steadily at the man. "No deals." Hennessey and Yellich had driven from York to Hull, never Hennessey's favourite city, to the Victorian prison on the eastern side of the city, near the docklands, to see, by arrangement, William Pierce. They met Pierce in the agent's room. Hennessey offered him a cigarette, which he grabbed hungrily. Hennessey then told Pierce that he wanted information about Toby Erickson. Pierce said he wanted to deal.

"Can't help you, then. I'll be a gaol-house convert good at volunteering to clean the toilets. That's better than nothing. At least it'll be something that I can take to the parole board."

"No deals. No promises," Hennessey repeated. "We can't make deals, we can't make promises, but if you scratch our back, we'll scratch yours. The parole board will be notified of any assistance you give, the more you give, the more you get in return. Especially if we get a result."

"So – what do you want to know?"

"Everything you can tell us about Charlotte Erickson's murder."

"He shot her."

Silence.

"Who shot her?"

"Erickson."

"Did you see it?"

"No. The first I saw of it was Charlotte Erickson's body in a deep freeze in one of the outhouses. Erickson showed it to me. Me and Davy Piggot. We were working for him."

"Odd jobbing?"

Pierce smiled an unpleasant smile. "A bit more than that. Erickson was into something, and we were part of it, something you boys never found out about, something that's no longer happening, but it gave him a hold over us. I mean, we were eighteen years old, scared of going to gaol."

"So what happened?"

"He said he'd shot her. She had a hole in her head. Right there," Pierce pointed to the middle of his forehead. "Little hole, but that's all that was needed. If the bullet didn't kill her, the cold did. The freezer was on a low temperature, he opened it up and this white cloud of whatever rose up, the cloud cleared and there she was – Mrs Erickson – with a hole in her head. First dead person I'd ever seen."

"Then what?"

"Erickson told us what he wanted us to do, me and Davy Piggot. Said he was going away. Told me to drag Mrs

Erickson's body from the freezer and lie it on the floor next to the freezer. He said he wanted her to warm up a bit. Then on the second day about nine p.m. I had to drag her from the outhouse to the flowerbed beside the front door.

"Davy, he had to hang around and put a rifle in a car that was to come. Erickson told him the type and colour. He said the driver of the car would leave the vehicle and walk round the house. When the driver was out of sight, he had to put the rifle in the boot. Gave him a bunch of keys. Modern mass-produced cars – practically any key will open any lock, the trick is to slide it in and start gently rocking the key backwards and forwards. Any teenager knows that. But anyway, he said the boot wasn't likely to be locked because the driver was 'a trusting soul' . . . that was it, what he said about the driver. Anyway, Davy did it – he wasn't really up to it, his mum made him go to Sunday school when he was a lad and he never recovered. He asked me to stay with him while he did it, so we worked out a deal."

"A deal?"

"I did it for his next week's wages."

"Big of you."

"It was, I could have held out for more – Davy was scared of Erickson, I could have held out for a whole month of his money."

"Even bigger of you."

"Well, Davy was a good lad, not cut out for the criminal life. I heard he got run over by a lorry – bad news that."

"You'll sign a statement to that effect?"

"Aye, if it'll help me with the parole board."

"It can't hurt you." Hennessey reached into his briefcase and took out a statement form. "Did Erickson tell you why he killed his wife?"

"He didn't even say that he shot her. But he must have, only ever those two in the house, and he took me and Davy to the freezer like he was showing us a trophy. Told us what he wanted us to do. Wouldn't have done that unless he'd shot her, or at least had something to do with her murder, would he?"

"Well," Hennessey took a ballpoint from his pocket, "if nothing else, this information will get somebody out of prison."

"Somebody's inside?"

"The woman in whose car Davy Piggot placed the rifle. She was arrested the following morning and she went down for Charlotte Erickson's murder."

Pierce paled. "I didn't know that, never knew that."

"How could you not know that? Don't you read the papers or watch television?" Hennessey was genuinely dismayed.

"I can't read that well, so don't write any big words in the statement, and the only television I watched was horse racing down the pub or in the bookies. And I left the area soon after that. I went away to get out of Erickson's grip, went to London but nobody down there knew who I was."

"Nobody knew who you were?"

"No. See, in Malton I was known, I'd walk down the pavement and people would get out of my way. I'd walk into a pub, straight to the bar and get served because I was Billy Pierce and I could give trouble, eighteen years old and I was *the* man in Malton. Thought Malton was too small and I wanted away from Erickson and so I went to London. But nobody knew who I was down there, had to queue for a drink, me! Queue!"

"Hard life you've had."

"Stuck it for a few months, see if they learned, see if things improved, but they didn't so I came back to the North. Never saw Erickson after that, not to speak to, never heard anything about anybody going down for the murder of his old lady, never heard that."

"She's still inside, eighteen years, Billy – and you've only done three and you're beginning to feel it."

"That's not right. That is well offside."

"You helped put her there."

Pierce nodded. "I suppose I did."

"Anything else you want to tell us? I mean, Erickson is not a nice man but there's still nothing to convict him of murder. No witnesses to the shooting and he won't cough to it, not Toby Erickson."

"That's all I can tell you."

"He showed you the body of his wife in a freezer . . . With Davy Piggot gone, it's down to your word against Erickson's and, frankly, he's got more street cred than you."

Pierce shot a cold glare at Hennessey.

"Look at it, he's a successful businessman, you're a lag with a string of previous and looking for a way to get out of a ten stretch. A jury won't believe you, the CPS won't even run with it."

"So what am I doing here?"

"There's honour among thieves, is there not?"

"Aye."

"So he's put an innocent woman away for nigh on twenty years. And he's made you a part of that. That's not part of the code of honour, is it?"

"It's not." Pierce shook his head slowly, "Twenty years . . ."

"So help us. You owe it to yourself, you owe it to the woman you helped fit up, and you owe it to Davy Piggot. You made it possible for Piggot to put the rifle in the rear of the car, and he felt so bad about what he'd done that he topped himself."

"Davy topped—"

"It wasn't an accident. Davy knew about the woman going down for the Erickson murder, he realised what he'd been part of so he threw himself under the wheels of a lorry."

"Oh . . ." Pierce held his head in his hands.

"And he's still out there; big house, pretty young wife, pair of flash motors, first wife dead, Davy Piggot dead, innocent woman still inside – all down to Erickson, so when is it going to stop, William? What can you do to help yourself? What can you do to help us?"

William Pierce looked round the agent's room, the two-tone wall colouring, the window of opaque glass. he looked at Yellich, then at Hennessey, and said. "All right. You won't nail Erickson for the murder of his wife, but I can give you information that'll help to put him away for a long time."

"Go on."

"This time we deal. I won't make a statement. I won't testify, not about what I'm going to tell you, you didn't hear it from me because Erickson has got some heavy, seriously heavy connections, really bad boys. Even in here I'm not safe from him on rule forty-three among the vulnerable prisoners. I'm not safe. If he knows that this information came from me, I'm a dead man. But in return for this, I want you to agree to put a word in for me with the parole board."

"No promises, but we always repay debts."

"OK, I know about Erickson, never saw him to speak to after I got back from the smoke, but like all the crims in the Vale I know about him. He's a rich man, he's got more than that property of his; he owns an island off the coast of Scotland, and a house in London, and I mean central London, and he's got one of the biggest gin palaces in Hull Marina. He doesn't get that from printing guide books and tourist maps."

"Are you saying his company is a front?"

"Yes. That's a good way of putting it."

"Drugs?"

"Drugs. Class A, heroin, crack cocaine. I hear it's brought to the Vale in pure, uncut form using motor coaches as cover . . . legitimate tourists wanting to see Olde Yorke . . . not so legitimate operators. That's what I hear. Don't know the names of the tour operators."

"I think we do. And he's still doing it?"

"So I hear. The criminal community is like a big village, it's impossible to keep everybody silent all the time. Well, I may as well tell you now, what me and Davy Piggot did. We were mules, couriers, but we were told we could go up in the organisation, had to start at the bottom, though, as hands-on couriers. If we got caught we took the rap, we went down, that was the deal. Davy got out, Erickson had him worked over – badly – but he said that was nothing compared to what would happen to him if he ever grassed Erickson up. Davy got the message and kept shtum. Me, I went to London, came back and Erickson left me alone. He knew I wouldn't grass him up, thieves' honour."

"But now you're giving information."

"Well it's not hard information, he's got a factory some-where – a barn they say – I've got no details of that for you. Anyway, he put an innocent woman away for too long, that's not thieves' honour – if you want honour, you give it. But this is off the record. There'll be no statement or testimony from me."

Upon their return to York, and Micklegate Bar Police Station, Hennessey telephoned the Crown Prosecution Service. The person to whom he spoke listened silently, but solemnly, and then asked that all documents, especially recent statements and interview transcripts, be faxed to the CPS 'with all dispatch'.

The red recording light glowed softly. The twin cassettes revolved slowly.

"I am Detective Chief Inspector Hennessey of the North Yorkshire Police, the place is Micklegate Bar Police Station. It is Monday, May the eighth. The time is fourteen twenty hours. I am going to ask the other people in the room to identify themselves."

"Detective Sergeant Yellich, North Yorkshire Police."

"Frances Copley, solicitor, of Brand, Copley & Nugent, solicitors, Lower Priory Street, York."

"Toby Erickson," said smiling, a smug you-can't-touch-me smile.

"So, Mr Erickson," Hennessey leaned forwards. "I understand you wish to make a statement?"

"Yes."

"Please go on."

"Eighteen years ago I killed my wife, Charlotte Erickson." Hennessey paused, holding the silence.

"You'll note," Frances Copley stared intently at Hennessey, "that my client concedes only that he killed his wife. He did not say that he murdered her." Frances Copley was a middle-aged woman and Hennessey could not fail to notice her penchant for jewellery, dangling earrings, bracelets and many rings on her fingers. She was also, he saw, very heavily made up.

"Noted," Hennessey replied. "So what did happen?"

"I shot her by accident, whilst cleaning my rifle. I pointed it at her as a joke. I didn't realise that it was loaded. I squeezed the trigger—"

"The rifle you shot your wife with?"

"I know what you are going to say. Yes . . . I reported it stolen along with a few other items. Classic insurance fraud. I needed the money."

"Then?"

"Well, then I don't remember much. But apparently I put her body in a freezer in the outbuildings.

"Apparently?"

"I developed island amnesia. I remember the accident, I have a dream-like hazy memory of putting her in the freezer. The next thing I recall was being telephoned in Edinburgh – I was at a business conference, it was the police telling me my wife was dead."

"How convenient – this island amnesia, I mean."

"It happens to be the truth."

"I bet it is. So how did your wife's body get from the deep freeze to the shrubbery in front of your house?"

"I don't know, I really don't. The hand of another is present, but I don't know the details – maybe I asked somebody to move it . . . the amnesia, I really don't know."

"But you let an innocent person take the blame. You stood by silently and watched her go to gaol?"

Erickson shrugged. "That wasn't the plan."

"I bet it wasn't. So why did you point the finger at her?"

"I didn't. The police found the rifle in Melanie's car after a tip-off, or so I learned later."

"Which didn't come from you?"

"No, not at all, of course not. Then the officer in charge, Mr Cross, asked me if Melanie had a motive for killing Charlotte so I said that she must have felt a bit bitter because I had rejected her in favour of Charlotte. He said 'yes, he could understand that women were like that', or words to that effect. You know, I never thought she would be charged on that evidence alone, and I didn't anticipate the weak defence, nor did I allow for a harsh judge. Then the appeal failed. Then it was too late, just a matter of getting on with life."

"And for Melanie Clifford? Was it just a matter of getting on for her?"

"I suppose it had to be."

"Eighteen years of getting on." Hennessey spoke slowly, menacingly.

"What can I say?" Toby Erickson sat back smiling.

"I want to know whether you'll be charging and detaining my client?"

"Charging, yes." Hennessey too sat back, and reached for the off switch. "Perverting the course of justice, interfering with the Office of the Coroner – insurance fraud. Detaining, no. The time is fourteen fifty-five hours. The interview is concluded." He switched the machine off. It was, if nothing else, another interview transcript for the CPS.

He accepted the offer of a mug of tea despite the heat of the afternoon. He always found it comforting to have something to hold whilst in conversation, if only because it gave him something to do with his hands. "The information is good," he said, "the guy is desperate to trade, but I want to protect my source – you know what these people are like – who can't make a statement and won't testify."

"No need for me to know who he is, then?" Detective Sergeant Liam McCarty grinned and stirred his tea.

"But it would be hearsay, anyway. He's not involved with the factory. I bring it to you because it's a matter for the Drug Squad. I'd like to see Erickson nailed for the murder of his wife. That won't happen, not now."

"But if he is the local Mr Big of the drug trade—"

"If he is, well that's a twenty stretch, right off."

"We've heard about the factory, George. We know it's in the Vale but have no indications as to its location. Coach tours you say?"

"One in Bristol, the other in London, that we have heard."

"Both ports. So it comes in in pure form, Erickson cuts it at the factory, sells it on in cut form to suppliers who sell it to junkies. So he's no small fry then, yon Erickson?"

"Not according to my source."

Detective Sergeant McCarty took the spoon out of his tea. "And your source is kosher?"

"Well, he used to be a mule for Erickson, so he says. Now he's taking on board the prospect of another seven years in M.S. He wants to be a free boy again."

"Sounds promising. It's often only the poor addicts we pick up, a supplier is a turn-up for the books, but this is an entire distribution network. Lightning like this doesn't strike often in a copper's lifetime."

"How will you handle it?"

"Only way we can, George, long-term surveillance on Erickson. He knows nothing of our suspicions?"

"Not a thing."

"Anything against him at the moment?"

"Perverting the course of justice, interfering with Office of the Coroner, insurance fraud."

"Could do time, that could work against us . . . we need him at liberty."

"Frankly, I don't think the CPS will wear it. The crimes are eighteen years old, and are based on his confession, principally. I think they'll put a red pen through it, it's very repressive to run with it after this length of time. So that should suit you."

"If we get the evidence we need, do you want to be in at the kill?"

Hennessey shook his head. "No, thanks." He stood and placed his half-drunk mug of tea on McCarty's desk. "Drug squad raids are for the young and fit. I'll see him once he's detained, if you get that far."

McCarty stood. "Thanks for this, George. In my waters I have a good feeling about this one. For a long time we have heard about a Mr Big, and we've been hearing about a factory for a while, and now you've dropped a name in my lap. So you won't hear anything from us now, no progress reports, but we'll tell you if we make an arrest or if the operation fails."

"Understood. The best of luck. I'd really like to see this turkey nailed for something."

Hennessey sat at his desk writing up his interview with William Pierce to go in the file on the Charlotte Erickson murder. After which he wrote 'cross-refer Weekes and information to Drug Squad – DS McCarty.' There was a tap on the door frame. He looked up. Yellich stood there.

"Lucy Gillespie here to see you, skipper."

"Lucy . . . ?"

"Cornelius Weekes' girlfriend, the school teacher."

"Ah, yes."

"She's anxious to tell us something. She's in an interview room."

"Couldn't get into Cornelius' computer." Lucy Gillespie clasped her hands together as she spoke, intertwining her fingers. "Kept trying 'til I realised that Cornelius' password was so obscure that only he would know it – like we said about a week ago. So I started to follow the trail, picked it up, spoke to people involved in the Charlotte Erickson murder; retired policemen, relatives."

"So you're the third reporter." Hennessey sighed with relief. "We had heard that a female had contacted people requesting interviews. We were anxious to find you, for your own safety."

"Well, you've found me. But I was in no danger, I wouldn't have gone to a remote place at night to meet a stranger. There was never any danger of that. But I've become convinced of Melanie Clifford's innocence."

"Yes," Hennessey spoke softly. "We are of like opinion, she'll be released soon. We're sending papers to the CPS."

"They've already gone off, in fact," Yellich said.

"Things will move very quickly from now, for Melanie Clifford, I mean."

"So Cornelius's death wasn't in vain."

"No, no it wasn't."

"That'll be a great comfort to his mother," Lucy Gillespie forced a smile, "but what a price to pay."

"Who did you speak to?"

"Anyone who would speak to me – two people refused,

a man called Cross, and a man called Erickson. I assume you know who they are?"

"We do."

"Didn't speak to them direct, kept leaving messages on Erickson's answer machine, Mrs Cross took messages for her husband. She told me that Mr Cross wouldn't talk to me."

"Did you say to either man what you wanted to talk about?"

"Yes. The murder of Charlotte Erickson."

"I see."

"Then at ten a.m. today I received a call at home, a man offered to meet me. I negotiated extra bereavement leave . . . he said he had information about Melanie Clifford's conviction."

"Can you describe his voice?"

"Male adult, local accent, short, snappy way of speaking."

Hennessey caught his breath. He felt his heart sink.

"So I came here. I don't want to stumble into my own murder."

"You've agreed to meet him?"

"Had to, had to appear keen, had to jump at the offer."

"Fair enough."

"We rendezvous tonight at two a.m."

"Cautious, if nothing else."

"He clearly wants it to be dark. We're meeting on Heslington Lane where it goes between Walmgate Stray and the golf club house. I have to wait by the turning into the golf club house. It's a lonely stretch of road and not well lit, but I'll be there, if you're there before me, waiting in the shadows."

"We'll be there."

"Can you show me a sign – for my reassurance?"

Yellich looked at Hennessey. "White plastic bag in the roadway, skipper, ordinary supermarket bag, held in place by a stone."

"OK?" Hennessey asked Lucy Gillespie. "If you see a white plastic bag in the roadway held in place by a stone, that means we are in the shadows. And we'll be there three hours before the rendezvous time. If the bag isn't there, don't get out of your car, just drive on. He'll contact you again."

"You think so?"

"If it's the person I think it is, then yes, because he wants to silence you, and his m.o. is to lure people to lonely places by offering them something they want. You can always say your car broke down or something but it won't come to that. The bag will be there, and so will we, and in large numbers."

"Cut it fine, didn't you?"

"What do you mean?" Hennessey asked quietly.

"You let me get my hands round her throat . . . I was applying pressure . . . she must have thought she'd been betrayed."

"Had to wait until you'd committed a crime, at least one that we had proof of, but yes, I suppose we did cut it fine, but we cut it. And attempted murder is serious enough for us to detain you pending trial." This, he would later reflect, was not the easiest moment in his career, but he had to hand it to John Cross. He was holding up very well. Seventy-eight years of age, a retired police officer of senior rank, with his life in ruins, his reputation evaporated. And not a trace, not a flicker of emotion.

"Better this way," he said.

"Again, what do you mean, John? What do you mean?"

"Well, if you've got to ruin your life, do so at its very end, less time to have to live with the regret. Better than ruining it at the beginning. Wouldn't have liked to have ruined it at the beginning and lived the rest of my life not able to recover from the self-destruction. That would be terrible." Cross paused. "I'm done for, George."

"I know, John."

"No . . . I don't mean in the eyes of the law, I mean I'm at the end of my life. I won't be able to cope with the cells."

"No?"

"No. I'll go with a heart attack, any day now. Once that cell door bangs shut on me for the first time, I won't have too much longer to live."

"I can't sympathise with you, John. You took two lives, you nearly took a third, and you allowed an innocent woman to go to prison for eighteen years."

"She's guilty." John Cross looked across the table of the interview room.

"She's innocent. We can prove that now."

"She'll get compensation, but I still say she's guilty."

"She's lost her sight."

"She's still got her life, more than Charlotte Erickson has got . . . twenty-seven years of age."

"Better than Donald Round and Cornelius Weekes as well. Why murder them? You could have given them a good kicking and left it at that . . . that's bad enough, but it's not as bad as murder, and they were at the beginning of their lives, just as Charlotte Erickson was. So don't get on a high horse about the murder of young people – you're in a glass house there."

Cross paused. "I'm going 'not guilty' you know. I remember enough to remember the good advice 'cough to nowt'. I'm admitting to nothing . . . I want my heart attack before the trial, I'll get buried in sanctified ground then, won't I?"

"I'm surprised that's important to you."

"It's suddenly a very comforting thought."

"But two lives, John . . . why?"

"Off the record?"

"Off the record."

"This isn't being recorded?"

"No, there'd be a red light glowing if it was, and even then there'd have to be a duty solicitor present before a confession was admissible in court."

"Never needed that in my day."

Hennessey remained silent, but the words 'more's the pity' entered his mind.

"Well, they had to be silenced," Cross said, simply. "If they'd been allowed to carry on, people might have thought I was wrong about Melanie Clifford. Me! Wrong! Never! Not a chance. Soon as I saw her, I knew she was guilty, you could see it, scorned woman . . . written all over her face, it was. She's guilty." Cross sat back and smiled. "All right, now go and get your duty solicitor and switch this toy on, but I warn you now that my answer to every question will be 'no comment'."

Hennessey stood. "No comment," he said.

WEDNESDAY
"There'll be compensation."

No reply.

"In the next day or two . . . I don't mean the compensation, but the trial. The compensation will take months, there'll be an interim payment very soon, though."

No reply. No movement.

"Your case will be the first of the day on the day that it is heard. You'll be brought up to the dock, you'll be charged with the murder of Charlotte Erickson. You'll plead 'Not Guilty', the Crown will offer no evidence and you'll be discharged from custody, on the order of the Judge. All over in a minute or two."

Still no reply. Still no movement. Still no display of emotion.

"I'll telephone your next of kin, so somebody will be at court to take you home." The Assistant Governor stood and walked out of the cell. At the door he turned and looked behind him. He thought that if Melanie Clifford could see, she'd be best described as sitting there, staring into space.

Epilogue

TWELVE MONTHS ON.

"They say that Dick Turpin was held in one of these cells."

"It's a myth." Hennessey remained standing. "The building isn't old enough."

"He was executed where York racecourse is now. The site of the scaffold was between the stand and the first bend. You can still see the bank where folk sat in tiers to see him 'turned off'. He spent half an hour talking to the executioner before he flung himself—"

"You didn't ask to see me to talk about Dick Turpin?"

"No, I saw you watching the trial, I want to trade."

"You've just collected twenty years, Toby. What on earth can you offer."

"Just for my own edification – your watching the trial meant that the Drug Squad operation had to be connected to your inquiry into Charlotte's murder, almost a year ago now."

"Almost to the day."

"So, between you and me, within these four walls . . . I'll tell you what happened to Charlotte if you tell me who grassed me up."

"All right."

"You will?"

"Yes . . . it'll give you something to think about. You first."

"I shot her. Deliberately. It was no accident. I wanted her money. Didn't want her."

"We thought as much."

"Read an article about a murder in the States, Florida, I think. The woman was murdered in her home and the killer turned the air conditioning full on, froze the crime scene. When they discovered the body they couldn't tell when she had been killed. It could have been an hour before the corpse was found, which was the time it took for the temperature in the house to fall below zero, or it could have been two weeks earlier when she was last seen alive, or any time in between. I had no air conditioning, but the deep freeze in the outbuildings served the same purpose. Got a lad — Pierce — to drag the body outside at a pre-arranged time, after I'd taken her out of the deep freeze a day earlier to allow her to thaw a bit. Phoned Melanie from Edinburgh, said I was at my house, asked her to come to the farm. She was always an obliging soul. Had another lad, Piggot, put the rifle in the boot of her car . . . phoned the police the following morning with a tip-off. The rest is history. How is Melanie?"

"Do you really care? If Britain still had the capital sentence, you would have lured her to a deathtrap."

"Yes, actually, I do care."

"I don't know any more than you do from the *Yorkshire Post*, six-figure compensation sum — still without her sight."

"Nothing more than that?"

"No. We do remain in contact with victims of crime but in this case, we were part of the great wronging of her. I doubt if she'd want police officers paying social calls."

Peter Turnbull

"John Cross . . . yes, he croaked, didn't he?"

"Heart attack, five weeks after his arrest for attempted murder. Not many at his funeral. So I heard."

"So it's your turn, Mr Hennessey. Who grassed me up? I bet it was that little snake Pierce. He's got trouble coming."

"It wasn't actually." Hennessey felt he had to protect Pierce. "It was you. You grassed yourself up."

"Me . . . how?" Erickson's jaw sagged.

"By walking into the police station with your brief and confessing to two minor crimes committed many years earlier. An inexperienced officer might have swallowed it, or a tired officer who'd been in the job too long. But I'm neither, and when you came to the station I saw a man with something to hide, offering us something in order to divert our attention from something else. So we started to watch you and we got a result, didn't we? Your factory, the entire network. Bringing it in with coach parties all over the north of England. All fell into our lap because you coughed to an insurance scam and an accidental death. Not bad." Hennessey stood as Erickson let his head fall forwards into the palms of his hands. "You know, Melanie Clifford told me once that she had calculated the number of meals somebody eats in an eighteen-year period . . . can't remember the figure, but it was quite a lot. Seven thousand, I think. Something of that order."

Hennessey stepped outside the cell door and waited until the turnkey locked it, and then escorted him to the end of the cell corridor. He went up a flight of steps, to the public area of York Crown Court Buildings, and stepped out into a hot, hot day in early May.

That evening he sat on the patio at the rear of his house, and squinted his eyes against a dazzling sunset in which a myriad mayfly darted and hovered.